It's Not Time
to DIE

Margarita Dager-Uscocovich

It's Not Time
to DIE

Margarita Dager-Uscocovich

Traslated by:

Glossa Traslations

Book design by:

Alynor Díaz / Snow Fountain Press

Published in the United States by Snow Fountain Press.

ISBN-13: 978-0-9981999-9-3

© **Snow Fountain Press**

25 SE 2nd. Avenue, Suite 316
Miami, FL 33131
www.snowfountainpress.com

Acknowledgements

To my family, beginning with my children Doménica, Joshua, and Anya for believing in me always. To Nicolás, my life partner, for his unconditional support in this crazy adventure. To Alejandra Otamendi for her unconditional friendship, to Luis Zelcowicz for his time and his words, and to Melanie Marquez-Adams for her words of encouragement and her valuable suggestions. To Pilar Vélez and Snow Fountain Press in Miami, for their professionalism and their trust. To my readers, my greatest appreciation for always being there.

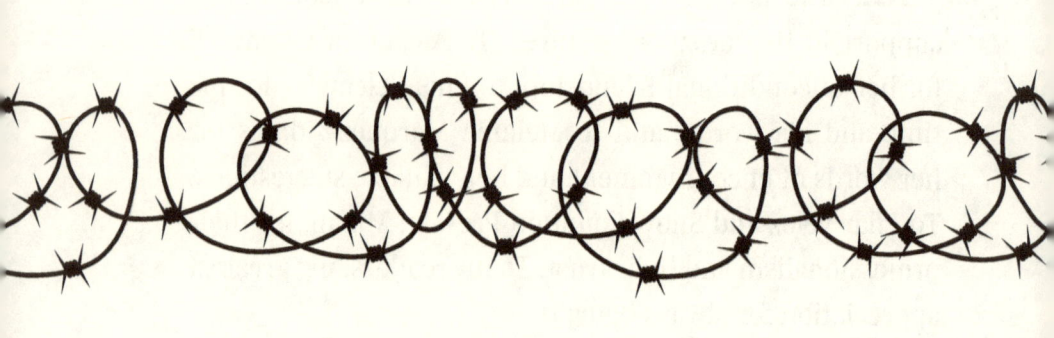

Foreword

Of words and wars

Poetry, like God, is everywhere. That has been its purpose ever since humankind took on the task of naming things and then playing with those names to give the world a life apart from the present one, in that other life, the one of shadows, the one of shadows that lives in the memory. Poets drawing a poetic side from the existence of things has been the origin of the harmony of art; the kind, natural, and sensitive side of the function of language. Now, to make poetry out of the horror of a war; that through the reading of a text grimly recounting how the life of a child like Keled, who barely dawns in his adolescence, first becoming blind in a hospital ward and then dying, irremediably, without Samira, his nurse and guardian angel, being able to do anything to prevent it; that, more than an act of poetry, is a miracle of life. Because that's what literature is also for. So we can discover that in the most atrocious of horrors, resulting from the injustices and the senselessness of war, there is also poetry and not just offering itself as a palliative relief, but rather as a shield, an antidote, proof that despite everything and against all the odds, during these absurd times of meaningless warlike confrontations, life will ultimately prevail over death. There will always be a wind willing to carry away the dark smoke of the fires left by the shrapnel and the explosions, and after each dark night, the sun will again rise with the hope of a new day. That is what we find in the reading of the novel: 'It's Not Time to Die' by Margarita Dager–Uscocovich, a potent medication against death. Reiteration page by page, image after image, that in spite of everything bad about the war and its horrors, poetry will always prevail with its charge of freedom and light. Through a courageous prose, agile in its construction and effective in the quality of the atmospheres that recreates its characters, from the counterpoint of the memory of a fertile and prodigious past, in opposition to an adverse and gloomy present: Keled, Samira, its protagonist; Nadeem, Baba, Jameela and Unjan, Hasan, Safwan among magny others, parade with an astonishing spontaneity, to tell us that they are as real as the word that they are meant to be. It is daunting that names like Syria, Aleppo, Zabadani, Damascus, out of a geographical memory full of sweet mysteries, become territories of terror in this text. There is no gimmick in this presentation of places and beings. They are so forcefully real and touching that you can't help but be thankful that someone rescued them from the record of adversity to give them a new life in a book that, hopefully, will reach many readers; because it has the great virtue of showing us that on the side of life, through the word, there is much to do and to create, that there are no sides when death reigns and that Samira's deed is the deed of all those of us who understand that our passage through earth is so fleeting that it can only be full of good intentions.

Notes on reading *It's Not Time to Die*
a novel by *Margarita Dager-Uscocovich*
by *Luis Zelkowicz*

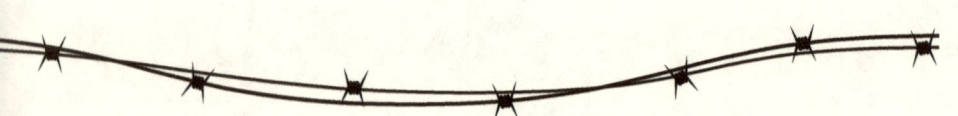

For most men
war is the end of loneliness.
For me it is infinite solitude.
Albert Camus

Death speaks

S amira is the woman with the sweet voice. She is beautiful. Her hair is a black cascade of light bluish tones that are further illuminated when the squalid light of the window rests on her head. Her curls fall in the middle of her face and, she ties them in a carefree ponytail. Her eyes are emerald green and her eyebrows are thick and arched. She is of medium height and her skin, slightly tanned, is splashed with freckles. She is an angel, as they call her in the Intensive Care Unit of Al- Hakim Children's Hospital in the neighborhood of Al-Shaar.

She washes her hands in a large metal tray and turns towards the man next to her dressed in blue with a sad and absent look on his face. As she dries her hands with a towel, she tenderly says:

"He went away with the ghosts of hope."

Samira refers to the child, whom she has covered from head to toe with a white sheet. The man in blue is his father. He has found his little one thanks to the lists that have been distributed around the city.

As Samira speaks to him, he takes the hand of his departed, squeezing it to his chest. No words come out, only sobs; his *masbaha[1]* tangled in his fingers and his left hand

---

[1]*Masbaha: a string of beads similar to a rosary. Traditional amongst follower of Islamic religion.*

over his son's inert body. I watch them. Eyes burning with tears. The father follows the steady footsteps of the angel who, swiftly, blends into the long, narrow hallway, leaving the faint sound of a song that talks about love, fear and the unknown roads. The father's gray eyes turn to me. He feels me. He knows that I am here and that I am the agonizing face of all the children of this endless war. He and Samira know that I am death and that I am hovering over them and that, perhaps very soon, I will come for them on a day as bright as this one.

Part One

Margarita Dager-Uscocovich

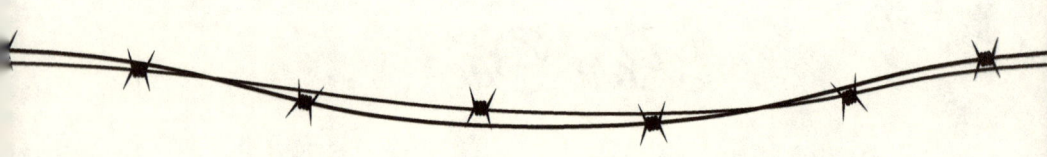

I hear the bombing and the planes; I shout "umi, baba!" The blasts are felt nearby. I try to straighten up, but I'm tied up. I shout again, more desperately: "umi, baba!", twisting in my limited space. Everything is dark; I can't open my eyes and that makes me feel impatient and angry. I have an earache and a sharp noise in my eardrum forces me to clench my fists so tightly that I dig my nails into the palms of my hands. I take a deep breath and the pain in my side worsens. A soft, feminine voice approaches, bidding me to calm down. I feel her warm minty breath overwhelming my nostrils. She takes my head with both hands and asks me to calm my nerves. I swallow my saliva with difficulty, feeling traces of sand in my mouth as well as the acidic and rancid taste of semi-dried blood in my throat.

My heartbeat becomes slower after the needle prick. The sweet voice tells me not to make sudden movements, that I'm injured, that she will soon wipe my face and my eyes. She stops talking to me but sings a song I recognize. It speaks about fear, about love and unknown paths. I begin to hum and make small movements with my fingers over the sheets, so that the letters may resurface from their hideout. I notice that my body becomes lighter and a perpetual calm invades me from head to toe; then I fall asleep again.

The night has passed dark and lonely and during that time I recovered my senses two or three times for just fractions of seconds. I wanted to cry but I got over it; I let the lightness of my body envelop me until the day made its appearance among clearer voices. I move my head side to side trying to accommodate myself so I can recognize the sounds; to make sure that the voice I heard yesterday comes back.

I hear footsteps from afar, still hasty. I hear tweezers fall on metal trays and the continuous beep of the machines; I also hear the labored breathing of the patients on both sides of my bed. I do not perceive complaints as in previous hours; I suppose the others are asleep.

In the middle of my silent examination, I hear the woman from yesterday coming towards me. Her footsteps sound different from the rest; they are light but firm and fragile tinkles, she gives off a soft perfume that travels from the entrance of the room to all corners. Despite my daze, I cling to the scent of her breath. She smells of happiness; I realize it when she talks to me and takes my head in her two hands. Between questions about news and some erratic chitchat, the woman with the angel's voice begins to pace by the room from right to left. She says hello and smiles; I know it by the nuance of her singing words. When she approaches, I feel her minty breath again and I immediately ask her to untie me.

"It's not possible for now," she tells me. "Be patient, you are very hurt, I know it's difficult, but if you hold still, your broken bones will heal faster. You spent two days buried under the rubble of a building. They found you because, in your semi-consciousness, you were whispering a prayer. The 'White Helmets' brought you here. I will untie you to wash you and continue changing your dressings in a while. Remain quiet. Rest will do you good."

She walks away with a firm step; then the room fills up with helpers who, like her, tend to each one of us who are at their mercy, wounded and lost because of an uncertain destiny caused by reasons that I don't yet know or rather that I don't yet understand.

I don't know how much time goes by until I feel that someone is keeping me company. In my solitude, I saw myself in Palmyra, running with my sisters to the sides of the ruins of the Great Colonnade and visiting the Valley of the Tombs, where children and young people like me, offer knick-knacks to the tourists or invite them to camel rides for just a dollar. I hear my father say "Children, there is the castle of Fakhar Ed-Din, look in the background, over there on the hill" pointing at it with his index finger, that looks long and thin like the branch of an olive tree while my mother sets her big black eyes over the horizon.

Suspended in the air, I go from place to place, observing how the stones of the surrounding ruins acquire colors full of magic in red, yellow and gold tones that give way to a majestic sunset. Suddenly, a light drizzle falls on us, appeasing the heat that takes over the city. They are tiny drops that look like crystals on our sweaty skin. Gently I return to reality, thanks to a stream of water poured into a container next to my feet. I feel the cold metal, it does not bother me. Instead, it calms the fever that emerges from every single one of my pores.

She takes my temperature and places a compress on my forehead. Then wets my lips and slowly unties me, lightly massaging the inside of my arms, my hands and my calves to activate circulation. I know she is my angel.

”So, are we awake now? That's good! “ The angel speaks to me. She has a soft voice; it pleases me. She owns a paused tone; the sound is harmonic and andante; it is similar to the rhythm of my mother's voice. She takes one of my hands, and with the other one, she taps me asking me to tell her something. She says that conversation is relaxing, that it will make it easier to forget the pain for a moment and allow me to answer a few brief questions that will help locate my family to let them know I'm in good hands. She asks me my name. I answer her faltering, licking the corner of my mouth and biting my lower lip.

“My name is Keled and I was born in Aleppo.” Immediately a sense of anguish and non-belonging invades me.

“I am in Aleppo, right?” I ask agitated.

She answers yes, and wets my mouth patting it lightly.

I take up the idea of the conversation again and I tell her that I was doing errands; carrying a small package to my older sister's house, not far from my own home. My sister, Nasira, is expecting a baby and we were going to eat together whatever little food Mother and her disabled husband had prepared.

Her husband lost his legs at Homs. When the conflict broke out, Zahid was returning home with a shipment of fabrics, when a grenade exploded in the middle of the road. His truck spun from the impact and ended up on its back, crashing into a light pole. His extremities were trapped and when they rescued him, his legs were hanging limp, revealing fragmented bones up to his thighs. He spent a long time in the hospital and we took turns looking after hi

While on my way to see them, a thunderbolt struck the ground in half in the middle of the road. I fell face down, got up, and fell again. I saw the sparks from millions of cement particles then looked up and watched as one of the buildings in front of me collapsed, spreading debris everywhere.

Suddenly, everything around me became dark. My stomach shrunk up and shot blood up into my throat. Then, I noticed fireworks flashing in my eyes with an incessant, hot and tingling sensation. I do not remember more; everything was compressed in time until I got here. I know I didn't get to my sister, I think I lost the package when the explosion was heard.

A long silence surrounded me. Tears strove to gush out, but they just wet my eyes. Feeling my mouth pasty and dry again, I asked the sweet voice for water. My tongue was burning and my skin was scorching; so, she gave it to me. I no longer felt the wet cotton, but rather a plastic straw with clean, fresh water. I sipped as hard and fast as I could; water spilled from the corner of my mouth.

"It's been a long time since water tasted so good to me," I mentioned, in an embarrassed tone.

"Keled, there's enough water. Sip slowly, I'll treat you to a popsicle once we're done with cleaning you up and checking you out."

I nodded and re-imagined the sweet taste of popsicles

that came to our neighborhood store.

"I love the lemon-flavored ones. Do you have lemon?" I asked.

"I think so," she said and wiped my face with a towel repeatedly. She also used oil-moistened gauzes to cleanse my eyes.

All those unknown faces, with their footsteps and incongruous voices, make their entrance, cooing us with their mercy, providing oatmeal and jelly. For a moment I hear guttural sounds and monosyllables that convey happiness. A cart with squeaky wheels stops near us.

"Keled, do you like oatmeal?" asks one of the voices.

Raising my shoulders slightly, I make a gesture, as if to say 'what do I care.' "Of course I like oatmeal, with cinnamon, like the one my mom makes in winter!" I think.

The sweet voice feeds me. I pause in the middle of each spoonful, I take a breath with difficulty and I tell her that what we receive for a month's survival is rice, lentils, pasta, chickpeas, vegetable oil, sugar, and flour in packages that supply the family, but there is no oatmeal. Rarely do we taste milk.

"You know, my father taught me how to make yogurt and cheese. We made cheese and yogurt together in my grandparent's kitchen, on the weekends, because it was more spacious. We joyfully made those gifts from Allah, while the women prepared snacks for the remainder of the day. First thing in the morning, before going to school on Mondays, we carried them to the store and everything would sell as soon as we would open."

Then I get a knot in my throat. I cough. A tear runs down my cheek. I'm crying, even though I had promised myself only to do so once the war was over.

She lightly pats my hand, getting closer to my ear.

"You are very brave Keled. We will find your parents. Now rest, I'll be back soon."

Then I stop her, gathering the little strength that I have left, and I ask her name.

"Samira" the sweet voice answers me. "My name is Samira and I am your nurse."

She wipes my mouth, picks up the plate, and walks towards the door.

I ask, "What day is today, I need to know what day it is. If it is Wednesday, I have to go, I have to go to WFP![2]" Concern invades me and the veins of my forehead swell. The blood runs through them, expanding them. My head hurts, but I speak loudly for someone to hear me.

"Tell me, please, what day is today?"

"Wednesday", Samira says. She is the angel of us all; a patient, wise, and kind angel.

Before I wasn't sure that they existed, now I know angels do exist! She is the angel overseeing the unfortunate lands.

"What happens on Wednesdays, Keled?" she asks me.

I answer, that it is my responsibility to retrieve what WFP distributes because Baba lost his identification and Mom stays home taking care of my cousin and my little sister. The war made my cousin Nadeem sick. When the attacks started,

---

[2]*WFP: World Food Program*

he would wet the bed. As the situation worsened and shots or bombs were heard, his hair and eyelashes began to fall out. Now all he does is rock back and forth with his bald head between his legs. He has seizures many times and falls to the ground, while threads of saliva drip from his mouth, turning into thick and large bubbles. Other times, he hits himself on the walls and moans, as if possessed by the Devil. He is my best friend, but since the war, the situation has gotten worse. We barely speak. His gaze is always sad and lost, and his smile, that was as big as a camel's smile with his slightly spaced teeth, has become a scary grimace.

Now that I'm here, who's going to pick up what the WFP give us? How will they eat? My sister is still too little to get out of the house. I must find a way to warn Baba; I must take care of my family! I'm starting to get anxious. I must force myself to open my eyes. I can't. They're stuck closed and the pain in my flank cuts off the air. The doctors say I have a broken rib. I cough. The cough is hard and constant. My ears hurt. I hear the voices distort again.

"Quiet Keled, quiet, everything will be fine. I'm going to inject a painkiller so you can get some sleep. When you wake up, I'll be here and you'll tell me more about your family. Surely they are well and will come soon looking for you. We've put up lists of all your names in the town, somebody will let your people know. Now, take my hand."

I do it. I cling to her hand and then Samira's lips brush my forehead with a warm kiss. Her kiss is like the kiss that mom gives me at night, to comfort my heart and scare fear away.

"I want to go home, my parents are waiting for me," I babble. In the distance, I can hear the blasts, and also the planes. Little by little the noises disperse and everything is silent again. I dream of the days before the war, those days when I played ball and dined in the courtyard, with the music of the box-drum that Fares played when visiting Baasima, my young aunt.

Baasima and Fares were going to get married in the spring, but the war came without warning and dismembered Baasima when a projectile landed in the mosque she attended for the last time.

My grandparents died too, and we found them a week later, hugging under the rubble of their own house, side by side. They were huddled together, as if not to let death separate them, but rather take them away as one.

Before, there was much laughter and, more than anything else, there was peace. I dreamt for a long time. I let myself be embraced again by the hope of days past. I felt the taste of the sweets that my aunt used to make. She was a cheerful and kind spirit. Baasima kneaded the world's most delicious sweets; her sweets of roses were special. She always made them in the shape of a heart, using her silicone molds. The neighbors predicted that her sweets would be the most famous of Aleppo and that people would come from all over Syria to buy them for weddings. In truth, her sweets were unique. There was something about them that made them exclusive. Although my Aunt Baasima was a bit older, she always had time to play with us. I miss her.

The days go by without major changes. There are moments when anxiety, tension and fright take hold of all of us, those who care for us and those of us who are here, immobile. There are children I no longer hear. Some have been taken to the morgue and others have been found by their families.

I'm still here, in pain. Not just because of the broken rib or the lacerations on my back, but because I miss my own people and I don't know what happened to them. The war continues to tread on me, it doesn't give me rest and I'm tired of waiting. I don't want to wake up anymore, reluctance stalks me, but I do it because I feel Samira caressing my cheek with the back of her hand. I feel her soft skin, her warm and gentle touch. She raises my head slowly to give me water. The water is fresh, tastes clean, like the crystal-clear waters of the rivers.

"What do you like to eat?" Samira asks me while she watches over me.

I suppose she does it to keep my mind nimble and to prevent boredom from taking ahold of me. Perhaps, so that I don't I forget how to talk. After taking a breath, with a little difficulty, I reply that I miss the taste of olives. At home, my mother always greeted me with a plate of olives when I returned from school. Back when we had a school. Now everything is in ruins. My school is just a pile of glass, rusty irons, and cement.

I frown, because sadness invades my memory. I clear my throat so as not to appear heartbroken and I carry on with a brave attitude. I tell her that Mom used to put them in a deep dish, with a splash of oil and a pinch of spices. I prefer black olives over the green ones, but I don't really mind the color as long as I can put a handful in my mouth with a piece of bread, soaked in the oil perfumed with the spices. I smile, reluctantly, and add that I also like the fleshy texture that enhances grandmother's stuffed eggplant.

Melancholy reappears and I turn my face over my right shoulder so that the trembling of my lips is not perceived.

"I'm hungry. Very much so. I would give anything for a plate of olives" I say. "Besides, I'm still thirsty."

Then my companion gives me a little more water to drink, with a plastic straw.

"Tell me more" she encourages me; "no one had ever made me think that olives could be so desired and described that way, now I crave a plate too. It's too bad they are so hard to find right now."

"I have not tasted one olive since the beginning of the war," I say.

I go on, telling her more things. I vividly describe my walks with Nazli, my younger sister, and how we went through the squares or nearby neighborhoods in search of leftover food when we didn't have enough food for the whole month because my parents shared it with families who had not eaten. How on the night of my birthday, I found a few potatoes. I had not seen potatoes for over a year, I don't know how they got there. I felt like a thief, I took them quickly and hid them inside my T-shirt. I buttoned my coat and ran home. Luckily my mom made us soup.

I tell her that I'd love to find a candy just to give it to Nazli, who enjoys those gummy jellies scented with fruit juice, stuffed with walnuts or pistachios. Her favorites are the rose ones. I remember when Baba returned from his travels, bringing with him a rectangular box, wrapped in paper of thousands of colors, filled to the top with those soft gelatinous delights that melted in your mouth. Nazli always shared some with me. The powdered sugar that candy makers apply on them, so they don't stick, left us white mustaches. We would eat a lot and laugh.

Samira prolongs the cleansing of my arms, my legs, and my feet, with warm wipes, while she listens to me. I take a long pause to enjoy the cleaning before breaking the silence. I mention how good the light foam feels on my skin and that I like the pleasant soft scent from the soap.

Engrossed in the goodness that sprouts from the hands of the woman who cares for me, the memories of my recent past immediately swarm my head. I sigh remembering the smell of flowers in the English soap that my Baba had in small baskets at the store. The same way I remember when my Umi used to dry the freshly washed clothes under the sun on the strings in the courtyard. The garments turned out to have a unique cleanliness and the wind that shook them turned them into small kites of different colors and sizes wagging in the summer sky. In winter, our clothes were impregnated with the smell of cedar wood, their texture turned firmer from the heat of the firewood.

But that was a year ago. Everything has changed. Now fear is hunting us, smelling us, chasing us at every moment with no truce.

I tell Samira that I realize I'm lucky after all because I have someone to clean me with water and soap. In Aleppo, water has also been scarce and there is no soap. When we bathe, my Umi wraps fresh herbs in thin cloths for us to scrub our bodies, to cleanse thoroughly. Many times, we must take turns and walk more than fifteen minutes to fill two jerry cans with water that last as long as a blink of an eye.

We use water primarily to cook. The humanitarian relief convoys were given access two months ago to repair the water supply in some areas of the city. We have little water, however my parents say there are almost fifteen locations, in hard-to-reach areas, that are worse off than us.

The moments of peace come in dribs and drabs. The days pass slowly, most of them immersed in memories and I am sad. If it weren't for Samira sharing her time among those of us who dwell in this room, I'd feel very lonely.

The bombings have continued, death comes and goes out of this first floor, spreading its acrid smell and at the same time so powerful that it hits you in the face. Yesterday and today, the room has been in chaos. I heard a little girl die beside me. She exhaled her last breath in the early hours of the morning. It was a deep and hollow sigh. She was exposed to the fire that occurred at the Zoco of Aleppo after an attack. Another child, in front of my bed, has lost his little arm and cries constantly calling for his mom over and over again.

There are tears that fall from the left eye, sad and empty sobs. My mother says that when we cry from joy, tears always flow from the right eye because Allah is with us.

They all come and go. Each day that passes the tension is more intense and the hospital survives with limited resources. The conflict is getting more violent. When the nurses think that I'm asleep, they talk about the state of the hospitals and of the families who flee, leaving behind a whole life and their dead and missing. The idea of my parents forgetting me, leaving to the borders, seeking peace without me, clinging to a fragile hope, disturbs me. I want to get out of here! I don't want them to forget me!

I begin to shout and cry. My crying is intense and prolonged; I can't help it. I cry because I want to heal the wounds of my soul, because I'm starting to hate, because I'm not brave anymore; because I'm afraid to die without looking at myself in the big deep eyes of my mother, without taking in my hands the hands of my Baba with his long fingers like olive branches, without feeling the warmth of my sisters' hugs .

I weep because in this languid solitude, memory drags its demons and the beauty of remembering disappears into this semi-darkness of cowardice and panic tinged blood-red.

It has been three weeks since the White Helmets' rescuer brought me here. Three weeks is many days. I want to get out of here; I want to see my family. I squirm and my forced darkness plunges me deeper into depression. I know I will never see again. A few days ago they checked my wounds. Dr. Hijazi, the attending doctor and Samira's boss, came and told me the truth. He said I suffered irreversible damage to my corneas during the blast, that the fireworks were the remnants of the explosives that collapsed the building where I was walking by.

When he told me this, I felt my chest getting crushed. I did not know the meaning of the word irreversible, so I asked him and he said, "Forever."

Forever began that day. I don't know what day exactly, but what I'm sure of is that I've stopped counting the hours since then. I no longer ask, I just immerse myself in this hopeless rest.

I'm only thirteen years old and I'm blind for life.

Before the war, I remember my homeland as vibrant and beaming. I remember the people who walked with ease through the streets of Aleppo; Burhan's shop, small and cozy, with colorful tables at the entrance for coffee or tea, where they sold delicious falafels, manakeesh of sumac and thyme and the kechek that Baba used to buy for breakfast.

We were all happy and wrapped in an immense and celestial sky, with the presence of a brilliant sun. We repeated the chores of our daily routines.

Aleppo was one of the most prosperous cities in Syria. It was a strong economic city, according to what the neighbors who were business owners and my Baba said. The city was full of kind and talkative people, who gathered in the boulevards just like the foreign tourists who studied at universities and visited museums. The ruins, the theaters, and the entire city were invaded by the sounds of different nationalities. There were markets overflowing with history and beautiful mosques over 700 years old. There were Christians and Muslims greeting each other kindly.

Now you can only hear war, which became a verb that embodies brutality.

I want to get out of here, I want to see my Baba! There is no one nearby, my screams evaporate, they turn to smoke in my throat and suffocate me along with my tears.

Suddenly Samira comes in. She recognizes the sadness on my face, pats me on the hand, asks me to calm down, and gives me a wet towel for my face while comforting me with her words of solace. With her reserved affection, she makes me jump from slumber to partial happiness. I say partially because I want to see my parents and my sisters; I need to know how they're doing and also if they'll be coming to see me soon.

Samira, my angel, has come to spread joy. She sits with a book in the middle of the room and says: "Today we are going to imagine we're Peter Pan!"

The few children that are left listen to her. I like her Scottish tale about a child who never grows up and who has Tinkerbell, a fairy with magical powers, as his best friend. They both live in the land of 'Never Never Land.'

The reading reminds me of Nadeem. I think that's what would calm him down and transport him from his nightmares to the happy land of make believe.

"Reading is magical" I interrupt her. "I read better than Nadeem. Remember how I told you about my cousin who has a big smile? I know I told you.

We both read every day, but he writes better than me. Grammar and spelling were difficult for me."

Karim, another one of the children, laughs with a soft laugh and Fatima and Mercedes, who have their beds in front of me, do it delicately by covering their mouths. I have learned to see with my ears, even though they hurt constantly.

She smiles. I know because the tone of her voice changes.

We ask questions and Samira answers us with infinite patience. Then she closes the book and sings us the song that speaks of love, fear and unknown paths. I can't close my eyes because they're hollow, but I am able to let myself be swayed by the lightness of the hope that appears in the murky moments together with my angel. I let out a deep and long sigh. I'm tired and I fall asleep listening to the echo of Samira's song across the room, along with the sound of bombs and the distant sound of planes.

I'm dreaming again.

In my dream, I am at the foot of an airy tunnel that separates the desert and the mountain. The aroma of the daffodils and the tuberoses, the lilies and the candies is refreshing, mellow and sugary. It becomes increasingly intense. The tunnel is ventilated and wide. I manage to see towards the end the lemon flowers and orange trees of my grandmother's house. I have a feeling that I'm going to see Allah. When I do, I will tell Him I like olives. He probably already knows, but I'll remind him in case he overlooked it.

I know He must be busy avoiding the misfortunes of others. I am blind, but I am alive; some died and others had to abandon their homes, wearing only whatever they had on. We stayed because we had faith, we had hope rooted in our skin. Now I have faith, but I don't know if my faith is powerful enough to work its magic. My Baba used to say, "There are people in worse conditions than us, Keled. We must be thankful that we are alive and well. Faith is what keeps you grounded and what lets you fly."

When I see Allah, I will ask Him to put an end to this conflict. I want to go to school and play ball. I want to run again with the kites, alongside Nazli and Nadeem, meet Nasira's baby, and play chess with Zahid. That will make him happy now that he doesn't have legs.

I hear voices right away, lots of voices around me. They are somewhat distorted. Some people run and others ask for help, but I can only hear the desperate hustle and bustle. A pressure on my sides takes hold of me. My heart beats quickly and then stops suddenly, causing a long sigh. The beep of the nearby machine turns into an everlasting sound that transports me towards a deep light that confuses me.

Dr. Hijazi told me that my corneas suffered irreversible damage, which blinded me for life; however, I can see Samira! She has emerald green eyes. Her bluish black hair falls into a split cascade on each side of her face. She ties them into a messy ponytail.

I see her wring the washcloths she cleans me with, letting thin, discolored drops of water fall into a metal container. She washes me slowly. The water is lukewarm and relaxing; then she hugs me and sings. Two threads of tears run down her face.

Samira lays her hand on my chest and covers me with a white sheet.

Margarita Dager-Uscocovich

Samira

It was Saturday, and I had been awake for more than twenty hours together with Omar, the surgeon on duty, looking into the eyes of the victims who arrived with their intestines hanging out because of the shrapnel. We had performed more than ten successive surgeries, deciding with broken hearts who would continue living and who wouldn't. Most of our patients were children, no more than twelve or thirteen years old. Innocents living a continuous massacre for the last three years. Nothing seemed to get better.

In the end, we ended up treating every wounded person who arrived, whether it was a child or an adult, a man, a woman or an old man. That day I was too stunned and exhausted to think, I wanted to go home, but the wounded kept coming nonstop. All I could hear was their deafening complaints. I stepped out of the operating room and I couldn't take it anymore. My legs would no longer support me and failed me. A constant and tenuous hammering pounded within my head, my eyes felt scratchy and dry, my hands were shaking and my whole body felt like it was crushed and broken.

I thought of my mother Naima, my sister Jalila, and my father, whom I hadn't seen in days. I needed to be with them, embrace them, feel the warmth of their bodies and the comfort of their words; so I could continue saving lives. I needed to sleep for a while, get cleaned up and have a cup of coffee.

The Russians had bombed Adr al-Haram hospital. I knew it when one of the rescuers from the White Helmets saw the planes over the building where the volunteer's headquarters had been. They knew they were Russians by the stars and red stripes on their airplanes, making them easily distinguishable because they flew very low. As soon as they left the headquarters, moving to where the first projectile had fallen in order to rescue the wounded, they saw another metal object falling from the sky growing in size as it approached its target. It was another rocket that ended up destroying the entire block. That's why they ended up there because it was the nearest hospital.

After the White Helmets rescued the few victims (I say few because the others disappeared under the rubble) toxic gases were spreading throughout the city, filling the sky with immense yellow-tinged clouds.

Some of those affected by the gas were moved to our hospital as well because Adr al-Haram could not cope. The children who arrived could not breathe, drowning in their own saliva, asphyxiating like fish out of water. When I stepped out to meet those who were helping people in front of the hospital, I saw a bunch of children, elderly, women and young people scattered on the streets trying to encourage one another; struggling to save those who shut their eyes, stiffened by the effect of the gases, which were painless but caused burnt pupils, vomiting and fainting.

I witnessed the event as a dramatic stage play, seated in the front row. The scarce medical staff asked the rescue members to help us because we couldn't handle them alone and they, the White Helmets, inside and outside the compound, were like ants sprouting from all corners, carrying souls sustained by a single breath. I observed as they cleaned them, calmed them down or gave them the last good-bye, holding unknown hands.

The members of the White Helmets ran through the hospital corridors, visibly tired. I also guessed that their spirit was exhausted, but they remained with us when no one else did. In a war where everyone took sides, they took the side of, and served, the disabled people.

The devastation caused by the bombings on those days was replicated inside the hospital. The deterioration of the health centers became the norm, part of the day-to-day routine to provide military advantages in favor of the government.

While I took care of the little ones, amidst tears they asked me if they were going to die and I said, "No, it is not going to happen today, be quiet, it's not time to die yet". I knew that I was lying to them because we could possibly all die that day.

The following hours were loud and restless, but we continued to pass the tests of fate. With every hour, feelings of confidence and expectation grew.

Those of us who were inside that hellhole, which did not

give rest, clung to that which we call longing. In the years that this unending battle had lasted, I had learned to read the fear and anguish in the eyes of those dying. People didn't die in peace. People died with the shame of having lost compassion in this life. Many did not die because of acts of war, but rather from sadness, anguish and desolation.

A month after Keled's death, our hospital suffered an attack that blew up the south side where essential supplies were stored. I don't understand why I relate the timing of the events with the arrival and departure of Keled, perhaps it's because there are souls who have very strong connections with each other. I don't know why I remember him so well, possibly he was my brother or my son in a past life; his mature and proper way of speaking; to reflect, to face up to the misfortune at his age, is what surely allowed me to engrave him in my memories. It is a remarkable feature of a previous life, as my parents would say.

Keled's story stayed with me, especially something that he repeated daily: "Faith is what keeps me grounded and what lets me fly".

Before the attack of the Russians, Al-Haakim was one of three hospitals standing; all the other ones no longer existed. The gravely injured bodies were transported to Turkey by the White Helmets, who were also victims of the bloody and disgusting reality in which we lived; first, because their families were dying and sometimes they were too far to rescue them and second, because they, like everything in Aleppo, were also dying. It was obvious, we were all, at any given time, at death's mercy. It was all a cruel and vicious circle.

We were bombarded twice in less than two weeks and the Al-Bayan Hospital received forty-five people, severely wounded in a barrel bomb attack. The director had to ask the patients in the waiting room to leave because the foundations were compromised. The moment after he did so, the building collapsed, swallowing the patients and one of Syria's most renowned physicians in the field of pediatrics.

We lived day by day, stuck between bad news and cruel actions. We received the news from the nearby areas, by word of mouth, from the patients who reached us; defying danger as they watched Al-Bayan disappear.

My hospital, Al- Hakim, was built in the summer of 2012. The day I was given the nurse position, I felt proud. I had finished my studies and it was my first job. Soon after, unbeknownst to me, I became a professional at the same time as the battle which started in July of that year.

As the attacks progressed, we had to move several times. Maintaining adequate help became difficult because there was only one accessible road between the eastern neighborhoods and the rebel areas of the province, which was being bombed almost daily.

It was Wednesday when I experienced the last attack at the hospital. The infrastructure on the south side was not only adjoined to the department where the medicines were stored and the pharmacy but also housed the neonatal unit. At noon, a strident sound pervaded the walls and the surroundings. I was in the opening unit to treat burn victims; the small area had been adapted to care for those suffering hand grenade injuries. First, I felt a swaying under my feet and then, the sounds of the walls in the adjacent wing crept up from the floor to the ceiling as they succumbed to the attacks.

Through the window of the room where I was, I saw the building gradually collapsing, making that wrinkling paper noise, only amplified a million times. I ran out to ask for help and saw the rest of the medical team scattered everywhere. One of the doctors on the floor, Hasan, came to verify that both the children he was treating and I were well, but from the expression on his face, I sensed that Jameela and Unjan were in danger. I moved him away from my side and jumped down the stairs to where two colleagues were. Suddenly, I saw the newborns wobbled???^wobble inside the incubators like fishing boats at the mercy of the storm in the Levant Sea. Some died from asphyxiation inside the plastic cubicles. When we managed to get them out, their skin was still warm. That image became embedded in my brain; the image of Jameela and Unjan crying, hugging the little lifeless bodies. The last thing I saw, appearing in my memory, was when both removed their colorful *hijabs*[3] and wrapped the babies tenderly. That was one of the most painful scenes I had to witness.

I walked in circles for quite a while when I left the

---

[3] *Hijab: Islamic feminine attire code used as a sign of modesty.*

hospital. I didn't know how to get home, I didn't recognize the streets, I was immersed in my thoughts, I was lost in a solitary world full of unanswered questions. A projectile fell close to where I was walking and the sound suddenly brought me back to reality. I felt hands that dragged me into an alley. All I know is that they were male hands, and they were strong. I screamed and kicked and used my body weight to free myself, all my efforts to do so were useless.

My eyes were looking for someone who could hear or see me, so they would come and help me escape those hands. I didn't see anyone willing to help.

In fractions of a second, I only saw bodies moving in slow motion going everywhere, running with their mouths open, screaming in desperation, with eyes wide open in surprise and fright. The explosion of another projectile allowed whoever was dragging me to let down his guard. I managed to escape and run the opposite direction of where I had come from. I hid in an abandoned house, behind big tanks that looked like garbage containers, waiting for the mortars to cease. At the hideout, I remembered the streets of my neighborhood in the old city when I spotted a daisy popping out of a crack in the asphalt. "How stubborn nature is; a flower that looks out on life surrounded by violence," I thought, covering my face. Then I heard another explosion.

That gift of color and life, in the midst of terror, pushed me to hide, with my eyes closed tight, in the zigzagging races that the children of *Al-Jdeideh*[4] had in the narrow

---

[4] *Al- Jdeideh: Historic neighborhood of Aleppo in Syria.*

streets. To forget the anguish of that moment, I clung with all my strength to the wooden doors covered in strapwork and the smell of olive soap that flooded even the tiniest nooks and crannies of my old district. The mind is marvelous. It reminds us of a feeling that was there, that you had forgotten, but that now because of melancholy and fear, it emerges, rescuing you for a few very short moments from the demons of war.

An airplane flew by very low and its sound brought me to the moment when helicopters and airplanes started bombing the old city. Within a week we had moved to a centrally located area, carrying with us my father's books, the beds, the TV, and whatever we had left.

The valuables had been distributed in our house in Brighton, on our summer and winter trips. Although it wasn't much, Mom and Dad agreed that it was best to move them if the situation became difficult. This was done along with the savings and other documents that Dad jealously guarded. Everything else disappeared in the old city. My youth became reduced to a pile of scattered sand. The firepower of modern weapons soon reached us in the new residence.

The old city was left in ruins the following year, in 2013 the whole country began to realize what it was to really live in fear. In the cities of Damascus and most of Palmyra, the battles between the Syrian army, the resistance forces, and the terrorists turned them into ghost towns. Everyone had fled in terror.

I remember my father pounding on the table the day our tiny television showed how the Crac des Chevaliers Castle, dating back to the time of the Crusades, was degraded to a den in ruins, because of rocket attacks trying to force the rebels out. The same thing happened with Saladin Castle.

With my eyes closed and the imaginary smell of olive soap, I broke through my nostalgia to the day when my father took us for a walk to one of his favorite places in the province of Homs. His private fortress, he would say. When I first saw it, I shuddered with emotion. It really was a majestic fortress and in the evening, with its white stones on a cliff on the plain, it looked imposing. 2010 was the last time I saw that fortress of high towers in all its splendor. It had withstood the onslaught of men for several centuries, now lying dilapidated at the hands of unscrupulous extremists.

The thundering in the air diminished. I had spent about an hour in my shelter. The anguish had almost passed. I retraced my own steps and made my way to the apartment complex where I lived with my family. I wasn't sure if I had a home or if my family was safe. Although we communicated frequently, and my mother or sister would drop some food off for me at the hospital when possible, I hadn't seen them in the last few days; I missed them.

The bombs, grenades, shells, and planes didn't go away. They stayed and often caused massive destruction. In the three long weeks that I had spent locked up in the hospital, I had ignored my own grief over and over again as I faced the fears of others, the scant recoveries and the unexpected farewells in a world of human beings sentenced to death. But in the streets, exposed to raw violence, alone and full of turmoil, I was beginning to fall apart from the normal reaction to panic. Little by little I began to experience the emergence of small scars that, with time I realized, would never be erased. One such scar was Keled.

Three years have passed since the destruction began in March 2011. The month of Spring, the month we all look forward to in Syria because the fields bloom and the mountains are covered in colors, together with the warm climate that carries the smell of pine. Women's Month and Mother's Day ended up being in the month where the tragedy of a civil war began with the repression, imprisonment and torture of children and young people who had expressed their discontent with the government of Bashar through graffiti.

Everything originated in Daraa, in southern Syria. A few kilometers from the Jordanian border. The level of violence increased from indignation to demonstrations, to brutal protests and bloodshed. The war to silence the people and to validate the continuity of a system based on corruption, intimidation and religious manipulation gave way to constant butchery.

The indissoluble feeling of uprooting and total discouragement began thus, with a complaint that displeased the Al-Assad regime. The rest was reduced to a life of distress for ordinary citizens, for those of us who were not in power, for those of us who believed that life was always a handful of good news. In reality, the world we live in here is a mixture of tenderness, harshness, disgust, and frustration.

When I arrived home in the late afternoon, after leaving my makeshift hideout, I found my mother and my sister embracing each other in a corner of the apartment. Their screams resounded within the four filthy walls.

"What's going on? Where's Dad?" I asked.

The two of them looked at each other and replied in unison, "He's dead!"

All the emotions I had within me exploded in a violent crying like an erupting volcano does. I never thought that one could cry so much, I never thought that death would reach me and claim an extraordinary man who had remained in a world where, for him, everything was amazing and miraculous.

My father was born in Damascus where he had studied Arabic literature and world history. He completed his studies at the Sorbonne and in England. He was a great professor, he always presented the best of Syria to the world; he loved living between two cultures.

We had a simple life in Syria and we alternated the seasons according to the Dad's itinerary who, between England and Paris, gave lectures in universities about Turkish invasions, the Byzantine Empire, Palestine and the First World War. For him, history was an endless tale with sparkles of satire, humor, ambition, extravagance and vices that were constantly re-enacted in the world. "One must be bold and sarcastic in order to live off of history, but what are we without it? Nothing more than a handful of cynics," he would say.

My father was tall, strong, corpulent. His reddish hair looked like whips of fire that lit up more on sunny days, sprinkled with freckles that took over his dark olive skin. He had a prominent nose, and his straight lips framed a smile with small teeth. Jalila, my younger sister, looked exactly like my father, and I looked like my mother. However, freckles had also taken over my geography, perhaps to perpetuate dad's memory in my body.

I remember that he never became discouraged despite the difficulties in the country. He was rather prudent and continued his lectures at the University of Aleppo, where he was highly respected and revered. Even when the country was plunged into a crisis in 1979, under the regime of Hafez Al Assad, in which Muslims were repressed, accused of being Zionist agents, he remained faithful to his routine. He kept a low profile, despite the powerlessness of not being able to help his students who were imprisoned or harassed, by the security services, for yelling slogans against the rulers.

He would tell us how many of his students died in the streets, by sniper fire during Hafez's time, and now the same thing was happening with Bashar. The bodies of the young people were thrown like garbage in the street and that broke his morale. But he never lost faith. Faith was a talent for my parents, but for my father, it was much more.

It was to believe that love is in everyone, even in those who doubt, since, according to him, it was not possible to live without a sense for the future.

Dad had been a witness to all these stages of repression, but his love for my mother and for the land where he was born was too great. He wanted to leave many times, but never did. When he had resigned himself to leave forever for England, to leave the cotton fields that surrounded us, the mountains overlooking the sea, the bazaar, the square and the visits to the Umayyad Mosque, the unimaginable happened: the civil war broke out, and he disappeared into the cold, empty darkness of his temple of knowledge.

The phrase I never prepared myself to hear, HE IS DEAD, resounded as the blinding grenades or barrel bombs did. It lingered like an echo reverberating in the ears preventing me from coming out of my own disorientation. At that moment my heart stopped for an instant, I was short of breath. The news hit me so hard in the chest that I couldn't breathe. I was losing my bearings.

"My father has died!" I said to myself, and my body crawled backward against the door, falling before the heavy news of misfortune. My mother and sister continued producing wild screams, repeating, "He's dead, he's dead!"

"There was an attack at the university, perpetrated by a terrorist group," my mother said, with a thread of voice denoting a disturbing emotion. It was a void where trust, intimacy and the freshness of our lives played a different role, a very distant one. It was no longer the sentiment of a simple life that showed in her voice, but an instated evil, a deep fear, a lack of stability that seized her from deep within. Her almond green eyes wept with melancholy. Grief spread all over the house, filtered through the walls, and took possession of the consciences and the body.

My sister intervened, sobbing, "but others say it was the regime that ordered two barrels full of explosives to be thrown. The explosion reached students and refugees who had occupied the facilities, fleeing the confrontation between rebels and government forces." Then, the three of us wept.

It was the first day of class of the semester and my father died believing in humankind. The comment of some witnesses was that their bodies flew into the sky and then fell all over the place. Blood was present in people's clothes and faces like an avalanche of red poppies coated in crime. Our neighbor Tarik witnessed the incident. Through him my mother and my sister knew that my father had died, then the television repeatedly played the video showing the fragmented bodies and the walls of the university, destroyed.

Many lives were lost the day Dad was killed. Parts of the Al-Lirmon area were affected and, in subsequent days, the neighborhoods of Al-Kalase and Salahaddin were bombed causing more deaths, injuries, and disappearances. People never believed that we were going to be bombed and yet it happened.

My mother and sister repeated, again and again, parts of the event at the university. Groans, tears, screams and reproaches mixed together. After a few hours, our tears dried up and we decided that the next morning we would leave Syria.

My father, so organized and cautious, had not arranged our departure from Syria on time and died leaving us alone with memories of the taste of arak, of family meals of roasted vegetables, stewed chicken and burghul; of trips to the flower festival in Latakia. He left us with the memory of a family united by love and dismembered by war. United by respect and by two religions that only professed one God of tenderness, of faith and of hope.

My father's name was Safwan. He was a Christian, but he was also half Muslim, something difficult for societies to understand. My mother was Muslim and somewhat Christian. They married in spite of their families, who felt that they would not be happy because their beliefs were not the same. Over time, however, they proved that love could do anything and that the acceptance of beliefs, inclusion, and diversity allowed the family to achieve respect. They painted their universe blue and lived out their dream of being happy forever, even though forever lasted only thirty years.

Before the war, our life was a constant mixture of languages, beliefs, and harmony. It was an alluring life where there were no dark spaces. It was full of light and smiles in a land that was very promising for my family.

The humble origin of his family, the fact that my grandfather stopped going to school to start working, defined my father and filled him with a sense of responsibility; he considered that the only commitment of the human being that is exercised with full conscience and freedom.

We wept for him. We never buried his body because there was nothing left of him. I missed him at that moment much more than in others. Time was stealing from me the space of his teachings, of his glances, of family conversations where he made us get lost in his stories full of excitement, sometimes making us the protagonists. I was partially alone, partially orphaned and could not process the idea of him not returning. I had no sighs left in my chest.

He made us better each day; with a word or a gesture, he could turn worry into joy; now only pain remained.

Sunrise arrived. My mother, still moved by the news, remained in a corner of the apartment near the kitchen along with my sister. The air turned thick and underneath that weird and rancid air, there we were, disoriented by the visit of the implacable death in our family.

I was at the foot of the door; I tried to stand up, but my muscles were atrophied and stiff from my position on the hard floor the previous night. Making a huge effort, I finally managed to get onto my knees and reach the end of the coffee table; I was able to straighten up at last. I looked out the window with a lost gaze; I didn't think of anything. I just looked at the orange, light blue and pink rays that mixed together giving way to the sun. Tears began to run again.

I noticed that part of the wall in the building was beginning to give way and the winter wind was blowing inwards between the crevices. I sensed again the heaviness of the atmosphere, I felt that the pain had entered through pores of the concrete, materializing in our house again, but this time in a more personal and furious way.

The sun arose gradually as the sole owner of the day, painting with its rays the depressing concrete skeletons that remained in the neighborhood. Fat tears kept appearing on my cheeks, but not with the same intensity of the previous hours. I woke my mother and sister and rushed them to prepare two backpacks, taking only what was necessary to survive the departure from Aleppo. I didn't know where we would go, nor what route we would follow to save us from dying like the others, crushed or scattered by a bomb or a grenade.

The only thing that was clear to me was that if we died, we would do so with dignity and away from a land that no longer had anything to offer us, a land that was taking away all that was good from us. I went to my room and took a bath; I needed it. I didn't know for sure when I would be lucky enough to feel the freshness of the water and the aroma of the soap. Besides, my clothes were itchy. The smell of blood and sweat resided in me. Grief overwhelmed me and the water certainly alleviated the suffering.

Minutes later, still shaken, I began to store our personal things; like passports, jewelry and the little cash we had hidden in our mattresses, as well as bottles of water, walnuts, dried fruits, candles, a box of matches and two chocolate bars that we found in the kitchen drawer. We rolled up three of the thin blankets that would protect us from the cold along the way. I took a first aid box that I kept in the first drawer on my bedside table. My mother and Jalila were silent, anesthetized by grief.

With a gaze filled with memories, I looked through the last of our life in Aleppo and of the family moments in our home. I went back to the room and searched the pockets of my uniform for the paper, folded into four, that Dr. Tayyeb had given me before he left for Europe. I put it inside my bra. When I left, the image in the living room of the two women who made up what would be my new life from that moment on, turned everything else to fiction. They troubled me more than war itself. So broken and so sad, they stood up and followed me.

As we turned and pulled the doorknob, we made way into a morning that, at the time, was not dangerous. As I stepped out into the street, I watched children play with an old ball. From their excitement, I assumed it was the only one they had seen in a long time. There was another child standing on a pile of rubble, distracted, flying a red kite made of plastic patches.

As we took quick steps to get out of the neighborhood, we would encounter young people on bicycles, staring at us. Later on down the road, I saw women with *niqabs*[5], women without husbands, with children and children alone. I saw elderly people, and people walking hastily towards the way out of the city with backpacks, suitcases, sacks, and bags. Some were barefoot or leaning on crutches, with concern

---

[5]*Niqab: A tunic that covers the head and the body completely, leaving only the eyes in the open. Its use became widespread under the influence of Wahhabi Islam.*

on their troubled faces. There were other people, with suitcases on airport carts that got stuck because of the weight or the rocky road.

Life continued, decrepit on either side and in front of us. I saw buildings that resembled giant ghosts with open and empty mouths, exercising hollow looks through their eyes watching us in a threatening way. Puddles of muddy water in the middle of main avenues that looked wasted and arid. There was dust, smoke, ruins, and the overwhelming stench of crime as we made our way.

We walked nonstop, the hours became endless; our feet hurt, and our breath was cut off by the cold that hit us in the face. We spent the whole day rationing the water and seeds. My mother silent, immersed in her own grief and sorrow, walked obliviously. Her gaze had faded, out of her shiny dark hair, weak gray hairs were born. From one day to the next her smooth skin, like that of peaches, dried up and cracks were visible on her hands. The memory of my father surely burned her skin; the memory of her big man was still fresh in her head. His absent love had become a thorn in her side that tormented her.

She discreetly watched my sister Jalila bite her lips, opening and closing her fists in frustration. She held back her tears to show strength in that eternal silence that announced the comings of multiple dangers. Jalila was the apple of Dad's eyes and he was her hero, her star, her best friend, the model of the man she would seek to marry. He was our world, our support, our example of success and he was taken away from us without having the chance to feel his embrace or his last goodnight kiss. He went to a plane beyond the light. Together we watched all those who walked those roads with hopes of getting somewhere, of reaching another border, be it Turkey, Jordan or anywhere that would receive us. Words were superfluous in those moments, the struggle of the battle for whom was going to keep Aleppo, made sure to leave us speechless.

When we left, I didn't know exactly where we were going, but we decided to follow the people leaving the city. After walking a few kilometers, we discovered we were heading for Idlib and I remembered that inside my bra I had the contact number of the person I should be seeking in order to leave Syria. From there to a new life I kept repeating; encouraging myself.

I had heard, in my days at the hospital, that those who fled from Aleppo and other provinces, where crime and terror were entrenched, escaped to Europe through different routes. There were several. Some were direct and others crossed a few borders. The relatives of those who had left said that the journeys were not always easy. On the contrary, they said the journeys were dangerous, risking dying at sea or on the bus that would carry you to freedom. In my case, since my father died abruptly, there was no turning back; I was determined to come out of the war and take with me the only family I had left. It was my duty, as the eldest daughter, to get my people out of that pit of pain that had changed our lives. War was a shadow of an ambiguous definition that haunted us fiercely. Whatever the cost, we had to leave; we had nothing more to lose.

Dr. Fuad Tayyeb, a pediatrician at my hospital, had approached me discreetly, giving me a crossword puzzle with the five escape routes to Europe. The easiest and most logical was to leave Aleppo or Damascus on a direct flight to our destination, but since the war had altered the natural course of tourism, there were no flights in or out. The other four routes were more complicated, longer and with a considerable amount of danger, at least for us as women travelling without the protection of a man.

He also provided me with the contact numbers of people who could help us get out of Syria; one in Idlib and the other in Lesbos, Greece. The numbers were written on a sheet from his prescription book; the black and fresh ink shone beautifully and dreadfully on the piece of paper, mercilessly torn from his block, to attest to a pledge among friends.

Fuad Tayyeb had been the head of pediatrics for many years, and we had to work together on days where one no longer counted the hours because we had no time. We had to try to save lives as quickly as possible. He and my father met during one of my frequent walks with Dad through the city. We enjoyed those walks around the neighborhood in our free time, but we also liked to go eat pizza at the Cantara restaurant, where lunch was calm and pleasant, surrounded by music. Apparently, Dr. Tayyeb also enjoyed it; sometimes in the company of his wife, sometimes alone. Since their first encounter, these two men liked each other and became best friends. The friendship grew, with the passing of many moons and for that reason, that taciturn-looking friend fulfilled his promise as best he could. Because the important thing for them was always, more than the act of promising itself, the fulfillment of the promise made.

"Samira, in case something goes wrong, if your father is missing, here are two phone numbers of people that can help you. I will give them your name in case you need to contact them."

I stretched out my hand, put the paper in the pocket of my nurse's dress, and then shook his long, thin hands. His hands emitted a warmth that reminded me very much of the warmth provided by my father's hands, generous and full of reassurance.

"Thank you, Dr. Tayyeb" I said, " I'll keep that in mind. Will you be leaving soon?"

"I hope so", he replied emphatically.

The doctor was an affable and dedicated man. After this exchange of telephone numbers, he never returned to the hospital. We heard that he fled with his wife to Europe. He did so after being imprisoned because, in one of the skirmishes between the regime and the opponents, he had helped the wounded on the street around the hospital. He was accused of treason against the country and the government.

Just as with Dr. Tayyeb, they had imprisoned hundreds of doctors around the neighborhoods and cities where the rebels were the majority. In Aleppo, little by little, mass graves were appearing with the corpses of those who were in favor of the humanitarian action of saving.

Through the hospital window, I witnessed on several occasions, how innocent people, mostly children, fell, machine-gunned to the pavement. They were not militants for nor against anyone. They were poor beings trying to hide from the violence of others or fleeing the crossfire. We were participating in a spectacle of consternation and trepidation that the world witnessed through computers and cell phone screens. Yet, no one beyond the borders of Syria and thousands of miles further, seemed to try to put a stop to that blatant genocide against not only the medical corps but an entire people.

Hands were needed to save the people, and the government prevented the doctors from practicing, locking them in dungeons. It was an aberration and I myself was suffering, but I also suffered for those who arrived wounded, for those who died and for those who fled to seek a better fate. In summary, many doctors left and we were unable to cover basic needs. I stayed out of conviction and pride.

I swear by my father's God and by Allah, that I was faithful to my patients until I lost my strength on that fateful Wednesday when the neonatal wing collapsed.

The surviving medical staff had to decide who lived and who died, inside the only operating room left in Al-Hakim Hospital. Every conversation about peace became stagnant, or slipped away, between the devastation of the great olive trees and pistachio plantations; accompanied by the only sound that became a ritual: that of gunshots and bombs.

After hours of relentless walking, we moved to one side of the secondary road on which we were and threw our exhausted bodies on to the wet grass; some on pieces of plastic; others on thick furs; the rest on small prayer rugs. The night soon came, and I delved into its depth. Its darkness connected me immediately to the image of my father. I began to cry. I cried from weakness and fear. I felt alone and disoriented. I knew I had to cry to empty my sorrow, to be able to start again and continue. Crying was the only form of relief I had in my possession at the time. When my crying subsided, I avoided doing my best effort, to think about what was unsettling me, so I began to play with the images of those who lay resting next to me. I created a colorful world in my memory where misfortune did not exist. I gathered all these people inside my head. I did it like a sheep keeper does, carefully.

Their figures began to delight me with their new expressions of happiness. Each and every one of them, came to me and took over my memory. I began to make myself feel safe.

In that memory exercise I realized that I liked the smile of the little girl dressed in pink, who carried her rag doll; she was sweet and sincere. I thought of the eyes of the boy sitting on his grandmother's legs in the wheelchair; they were indigo blue, small, and the irises carried marks of sadness.

The colors of people's clothes transported me to Keled's story, the one he told me in the hospital, about clothes hanging in the sun, moving like kites in the afternoon breeze. These clothes also moved with the gusts of winter wind. There were glowing yellows, invigorating oranges, pompous reds, and fresh greens; there were magisterial blacks and deep blues. I smiled. The cold continued lashing at the body, and the neighboring voices started to fade. I fell into a deep sleep despite the icy wind that was getting into my lungs; breathing was turning into a blunt action.

The sleep effect was short-lived as airplanes and helicopters began to fly in circles in the sky. Another attack. We had just left Aleppo behind us and were facing, not far from where we were camping, the aftermath of a possible assault.

I woke up stunned, listening to my mother's voice asking for calm and shaking me to wake up. My head felt heavy, I listened to the women consoling the children who were confused, just like me. I tried to stand up, but my body was dizzy; I tripped and fell, then I knelt and saw several fireballs falling from the sky. One of the fireballs fell and the tremor of the earth felt so strong that we thought it would open under our feet, swallowing us all. I could hear screams of terror.

My mother rocked Jalila, asking her to wake up. Her voice sounded like when we were children: determined and quick. When she gave an order, the sense of urgency sailed steadily and affectionately. "Wake up Jalila, wake up, I think they're going to kill us, wake up now!" Suddenly both of us stood up, bewildered by the infernal sound of human moans and iron birds around us.

The men that were with us rushed to collect their belongings and cover the most helpless, dragging them to a deeper area of the road, where there were large rocks. Several trucks pulled over at the side of the road, near where we slept. A group of soldiers got off carrying high caliber weapons. Some moved around and others came towards us bearing emaciated faces. I realized that some of them had been the faces of children. Not long ago they might have been on the street playing soccer or riding a bicycle through the neighborhood, with a dream on their minds. But at that moment their skin looked worn out. Their dilated eyes announced terror and we, between the screams and the cries, between the gloom and the lights of the trucks, experienced the same feeling.

The soldiers demanded immediate identification, with an emphasis on checking the men's identification. Nervousness was noticeable in their gestures. I told my mother to hide our passports and leave only the identification cards. The money we had, I stuffed inside our panties, and Jalila hid our few jewels behind the nape of her neck, inside her hijab. We had no idea why they wanted our identifications, but it was better not to ask or resist; it was not worth it. The three of us hugged together hoping that nothing unfortunate would happen; it was too much to ask.

Two men approached us. They were kind. They asked us not to be frightened, but the situation itself caused the aversion that comes with anxiety. They said they were members of the rebel army.

"There's nothing to fear, we won't hurt you", said the tallest man.

"Don't worry, we have nothing to hide", replied my mother in a stern voice, issuing our identity cards.

The man didn't take them, rather he smiled slightly. My legs were shaking. My sister grabbed my hand too hard, hurting me. Hugging me, my mother kept digging her fingertips on my left shoulder, causing an uncomfortable pressure.

It didn't make much difference to me whether they were from one army or another. Being in the rebel army was no guarantee of security because the Islamic rebel army had associations with branches of more than a thousand small armies, made up of civilians, in which terrorists were infiltrated. Knowing who was good and who would harm us was almost impossible.

The soldiers passed in front of us, with their backs to the birch trees whose branches moved to the rhythm of the night wind. They went directly and steadfastly towards the other group where the other men of our caravan were, yelling for the men to uncover their faces and identify themselves. The friendly voices became harsh.

The soldiers compared the faces of the travelers with pamphlets they had in their hands. Their voices became threatening causing four kids to run away in less than a minute. "Stop them, stop those sons of bitches!" I didn't know where the voice came from; only the women's cries and the children's weeping were heard. We closed our eyes and held each other much tighter, almost turning into one body. We felt our warm breaths filling our reduced space; the heartbeats, so powerful, that I could hear them loudly. Shots were fired and then silence enveloped the earth and the bodies that fell.

The soldiers returned with their heavy weapons, brushing their bulletproof vests. The noise produced by that friction rattled me as if a thousand invisible swords cut through the air. With the adrenaline rushing through their bodies, they aimed at all of us who were scattered along the wet grass. Before my eyes, the kindness with which they had spoken to us, in the beginning, became an ultimatum in which they made it clear to us that cowardice should not be rewarded; that if there was another opponent to the true freedom of Syria, they would find him and kill him.

The uniformed men shouted in unison, "*Inshallah, Inshallah!*[6]" The shots were aimed at the dark immensity of the dome above our heads which, like paper-maché, was filling with cracks from the bursts of fire crossing each other.

Squeezing Jalila's and my mother's hands, I thought they were going crazy. A slight burning sensation appeared invasively, climbing from my stomach to my esophagus provoking that a gulp of sour, greenish water emptied onto the grass; I gagged twice more. I felt my body fall backward as the whimpers of my mother and sister became distant and inaudible. It was then that I saw death up close and heard its voice in whispers. By my side, she was direct and immutable telling me new stories.

---

[6]*Inshallah: Arabic expression meaning, "So be it".*

We never knew if those four young men, machine-gunned at dawn, were actually trafficking information on behalf of the government or someone else. We put rocks on top of rocks, and they were trapped forever in a cold, deserted, and perhaps, unknown field. They were buried as martyrs, without a flag, but with the *Tekbir*[7] and singing over their graves "Shahid habib Allah." After the burial, the *Fatiha*[8] was prayed and we walked away from them, counting the forty steps for the angels to attest to their faith.

The vileness of the rebel attacks, of the Syrian air forces, of the Russian allies, continued to be felt through the secondary roads. I walked always absorbed in my heartbeat which slowed down for brief moments. There was a crowd wandering, lost in their memories, whose new faces joined our caravan. No matter the time of day or night, strangers became close as they told their stories. I think that by telling them, they thought the horror would disappear from their lives. Talking about their losses became therapy, even for the youngest ones. We couldn't tell ours yet. It was too fresh and it hurt.

There were children's voices behind me that got me out of my thoughts. One of them, the youngest one, remembered how his friend Alide, just ten years old, died when a rocket exploded at his school. "It all happened very fast," said the boy with roguish eyes and dark hair. "Alide had turned around to pick up the ball that slipped across the courtyard during recess, and I saw his body explode against the wall.

---

[7]*Tekbir: Expression of faith in Islam widely used in the Muslim world.*
[8]*Fatiha: The first of the chapters into which the Qur'an is divided.*

When he fell to the ground his head was shattered."

I closed my eyes and felt his warm blood sticking to my flesh. I didn't move. I looked at him taking over part of his grief and extended my hand to comfort him. His little companion, another boy, almost his own age with amber eyes, ran his arm over his shoulders without uttering a word. It was an innocent and warm act. He ended up saying, almost in a whisper, that they could recognize Alide by the shoes that had the flag of his favorite Spanish soccer team, Barça; his aunt had sent them to him as a birthday present.

Mohammed was another boy whose thirteen-year-old cousin had been captured in Homs. They tortured him by burning him with cigarettes, leaving him without food or water for a week. The boy with the amber eyes narrated, in a faltering voice, how a fifteen-year-old boy was hung from his thumbs on the roof of the school, all because he did not want to be part of extremism. He had died of a heart attack due to the abuse.

Along the way, I listened to stories wrapped in tragedy and my heart shrank with each of them. Every word I heard plucked silent tears from me. The last dark stories that I allowed myself to lend my ears to, were those of one mother telling another, between sobs, that the dead children in her province lay in piles in the street in broad daylight; in full view of passersby. Dogs fed on them. Outside her house, those bodies covered with blood and sand chased her every moment. She said that when she slept or ate, they were there, like ghosts, reminding her that she was a mother.

She thought it best to leave with her son before he ended up, by fate, being food for rabid dogs. But even far away, the smell of putrefaction and abandonment stuck to her body. The images of the corpses out in the open drove her mad, plunging her into a deep and restless sadness. She was certain that she would lose her mind at any moment. The burden of the deceased was very heavy.

Faced with these revelations, I wondered what the people of my village were made of. It was my people, it was my country. A whole state divided and, consequently, dying under a barbaric attack that had gone viral.

I had lived in a bubble. My life had not been miserable, on the contrary, my life was comfortable and full of happy moments. However, in these moments I was experiencing misery. Not of economic scarcity, which was what worried me the least. I was at the door of a worse kind of misery, more cruel and merciless, more vain and perverse. Human misery was pushing us towards unknown paths of inexorable pain.

We kept walking. Temperatures began to plummet. The cold wind was a wave loaded with white flakes, drilling into the bones. We still had a long way to go until we reached Idlib. I heard Mustafa, a grandfather pushing his wife's wheelchair along with his orphaned five-year-old grandson, tell his family that they would soon be safe, that there was nothing to worry about, that they had to keep the faith. On hearing that phrase, "Keep the faith," I immediately remembered Keled.

Before he died, he said that his Baba told him that faith was what kept him grounded and what let him fly. Then my heart shrunk and a sigh, traveling from my stomach, escaped from my mouth to meet the wasteland of Highway 60. Mustafa looked at me, smiling sadly. I would say that his smile was rather absent. What was drawn on his lips was a grimace, covered with shame and disgust, but above all, full of ghosts. Pain was haunting him, so he decided to tell me his story. Slowly and deliberately and with his eyes staring into infinity, he said that his son Ibrahim, and his wife Aisha, died the year before, the day after Bashar's regime and his people celebrated Christmas. While the other half of Aleppo and the whole of Syria were being destroyed, robbed, and machine-gunned, he witnessed the laughter, the dancing and the posters of Putin's face hanging from and posted on houses and vehicles. His face became tense during the conversation. He said that a handful of men and women were celebrating, and he was wondering, "Does it not reek of death to them? Is it that they have no compassion, no shame?"

Feeling repulsed and upset, he returned to his home in the neighborhood of Tariq al-Bab. The next day, bad luck knocked on his door, announcing the death of his only son and daughter-in-law. During a confrontation between the rebel forces, Islamics, and the Syrian army, heavy artillery was unleashed in the area, taking over the road to the city's airport. His relatives had gone to receive food supplies that morning and death ruthlessly claimed their lives. Their daughter-in-law died of a broken neck with her son. Half of his body had been crushed by the wall of the building across from them. Those who survived began to dig up the wounded with their hands, until their fingertips turned to blood and their nails fell off.

Mustafa's eyes filled with tears, and his thick voice was fading with the pain of memory. He then leaned with both hands on the wheelchair handles and wiped his face with the sleeve of his sweater. "Forgive me. The conversation took me by surprise. I thought I was over it, but, as you see, it is not so." His wife stroked his hand and kissed the forehead of his grandson who lay in her arms numb from the cold and exhaustion. The little one was traveling wrapped in an old sheepskin.

We advanced a few more kilometers and night fell again. We found a farmhouse and our bodies were crying out for rest. It was very cold and our bones were cracking; our bodies trembled uncontrollably. We went inside and settled amid the rubble. My mother still didn't speak, and my sister still had her fists clenched. I was hitting rock bottom.

We took off our backpacks and helped Mustafa and his family settle in along with some of the displaced people who were with us. With the few dry branches and some old sticks we, made a small bonfire, so small that it showed signs of extinguishing quickly. We managed to warm the hands and bodies of the ten children who were traveling with us. There wasn't much we could do, but we tried.

Jalila rubbed the children's hands and feet to stimulate blood flow. For a moment they forgot about their own cold and between weak smiles, they began to caress their little limbs. Then they did it to each other. My mother put them to bed as close as possible to each other so that they would get warm, covering them with our scrawny bedspreads. Their faces recovered their calm during sleep.

The night dragged on. The adults could not completely fall asleep, and the rats interrupted their few seconds of peace. Some were coughing, others were sobbing; others were so tired that their intermittent snoring sounded like the chronic echoes of a high-volume nightmare. Near the makeshift bonfire, the chattering of some women's teeth could be heard. Fear haunted us, stalked us without mercy. My throat felt like a triple knotted rope. I wanted to hold back the tears that filled my eyes by looking up, but when I saw before me the bright, round moon over that black, icy, infinite firmament, I let them out with no shame.

At a distance, there was still war. Bursting noises resonated from the sky; red flashes of light fell that later generated incalculable clouds of smoke and earth. The temperature cooled. My mother and my sister slept. They all slept or tried to. I spoke to myself with the bonfire, the moon and my tears as witnesses. Alone, with my many feelings, I recapped time and realized that it was December already, that Aleppo was being left behind and that its distance burned beneath my feet.

On foot, Aleppo was thirteen hours away from Idlib. Unfortunately, it had taken us much longer to get there. Sixty kilometers separated us from our new destination. Only sixty kilometers more to be able to contact and negotiate with that faceless voice; that voice identified by a series of numbers in black ink that I kept between my breasts. I sighed and ran the palms of my hands over my eyes. I made myself as comfortable as I could in a corner, that briefly, isolated me from the rest. "Right now, the world is still going on for all we know," I said to myself, and I closed my eyes until the next day.

I awoke with swollen eyes. Mustafa made tea and my mother shared the chocolate bars with some of the children. "There's not enough for everyone," she said, and she handed out seeds and some dried fruits. We all shared what we had: tea, bread, honey or dates. We set off again. It was only a few kilometers to Idlib. Once again, we were walking, spurred on by inertia, especially I, accompanied by the same feeling of concern I had when I left my house in Aleppo and which had not abandoned me during the last few hours.

The scenery didn't help much. We could only glimpse land covered by a light layer of snow from the previous night. From time to time, arid potholes appeared before our eyes like the few birch and oak trees that were hiding part of their greenness. An old and dilapidated building, falling apart here or there, would bid us farewell as we passed.

Just like that, it started drizzling and there was nowhere to go for cover. The drops splashed us spiritedly, our clothes were beginning to stick and hung from us by their own weight. We continued walking, and the blades of grass transmuted into small condensed flakes that, like cotton, settled on our heads. With much effort, we were reaching Idlib.

As we entered the city, a shadow covered the buildings like a postcard; where evil and self-interest stipulated what was good and what was bad, all under one color. Through the crowds, we could see walls hanging from their houses, mountains of rubbish in the corners, and scraps of clothing in the streets. A combination of misery and signs of shattered dreams. Among them, the snow and the mud received us in a precarious party.

Mustafa was very tired. His grandson was a lump stuck to his grandmother's chest, he was turning purple from the cold and only slept. Laila with her swollen knee, green with pain, only wiped her snot with the tip of the shawl that covered her gray hair. She moaned bitterly from the discomfort and unease in which she traveled. It was understandable; although her complaints did not help, they only made us more tense. It was impossible to avoid, just necessary to bite the bullet and continue. My mother, Jalila and I took turns pushing the chair and carrying the child along the route.

Mustafa began to raise and lower the beads of his masbaha with the fingers of his left hand. I suspected he was anxious. I saw him deteriorate by the minute. I began to imagine that Mustafa's smile must have been a broad, resounding smile. His blue eyes, like the Levantine sea, must have had the brightness of the sky on summer days. His gaze was always lost and his eyes became opaque like the mist that appeared at night.

Chaos also reigned in Idlib. There were vehicles forming

long queues in the middle of the streets, where there were not only lost pedestrians going through and hauling children, but also limping dogs and agitated cats, as well as trucks with soldiers invading the opposite lanes or skirting around the ruins of fallen buildings. There were also the displaced, those in appalling humanitarian condition who came to invade the province. We were a river of helpless people seeking to escape the bombs that, continuously, stalked us in our own not so faraway lands.

The voice of a member of the White Helmets, who passed by my side, brought me back to reality when I heard him say: "This province will be the next Aleppo if the Islamic rebels, Bashar's regime, and the Russians do not reach an agreement." He scratched his head in annoyance, carrying his helmet in his right hand. His coldness made me impatient. A man with curly hair, and a beard painted white by the snow that clung to it, appeared beside him. His gaze was deep and something in it told me that very soon destiny would put him in my way. It was a feeling of comfort; I floated, for a moment, towards his space. It was strange but pleasant. Confusing. But his eyes gave me confidence.

The word PRESS on his vest gave me the excuse to dare and ask about the help that was needed. I approached and babbled, "We need a doctor, do you know where can I get a doctor?" He continued staring at me and pointed to the other side of the road with his index finger. His masculine, round, and pleasant voice translated into clear directions.

I thanked him and we crossed the street, avoiding the

people who continued to emerge uncontrollably from all corners of the city. Something drove me to turn around to the avenue behind me and there he was, with his chocolate eyes, looking at me silently and intensely. A passing vehicle drove us away from each other. We both disappeared between the crowds and the hustle and bustle of the streets.

Some of our walking companions began to disperse, with their few belongings, to the homes of the relatives who would house them; others stayed with me as if I were a messiah, as if I had the solution to everything.

I must say that I used to like the snow but now it scares me. It evokes in me a feeling of displacement and infinite loneliness.

My sister and my mother, like the elementary school teachers they were, led the four children who stayed with us, in a single line, towards the location that had been indicated to me. I made way with my hands so that the vehicles wouldn't run us over. The city was not in good condition either but it was better than when we left Aleppo. We found help for Laila, her grandson Hakim, and the five other adults who were dragging their feet, at the last International Medical Organization of France Assistance Center.

The director of the center introduced himself as Claude Mirren. I watched his hands. He was a man with thick hands that took possession of mine in an honest and warm handshake. I perceived it immediately as I greeted him. His height reminded me of the Malwiya Tower in the Great Mosque of Samarra in Iraq, when we went on a family trip before starting work at the hospital. He welcomed us along with a few members of his team: three women and two men who looked exhausted. All six had deep dark circles and prominent bags under their eyes, but neither the fatigue nor the loneliness of war prevented them from approaching and welcoming us as the parents of prodigal sons do.

Soon, Dr. Claude gave orders to take care of the children first, and he personally took care of Laila's swollen, purulent knee. When he removed the bandages, the smell was strong and rancid; the knee was gangrenous. He asked me to stay to interpret and that's how I found out that he and his doctors were going to Turkey. They had lost staff, patients, and ambulances. They could no longer assist the pregnant women and the vaccines for the children had been stolen days before.

His mood wasn't down, but he was aware of his limitations. Without enough staff and medicines, he couldn't do much. "There are days when all the effort to save lives becomes a daunting task," he said while cleaning scrapes and sterilizing instruments.

The Fatah al-Sham Front had murdered one of its doctors. He said she was a Syrian-English colleague who was on her way to Turkey with a critically ill patient. They had only three days of water and three days of light and all the chaos of war was putting his sanity and his Hippocratic oath to the test. When at times I heard his voice fading, I said: "I am a nurse, I worked at the Al-Hakim Hospital in Aleppo, I can help."

"Yes, help us!" was his immediate reply, "I can't pay you, but we can't manage on our own anymore." He hugged me tightly, almost squeezing my bones. The contact with the skin of another human being in such a direct way offered in those tragic moments comfort, security, and protection. I felt its warmth again and this time it remained, traveling over my skin, comforting and reviving me, even though my clothes were wet from rain and snow.

It seemed that, like me, Claude Mirren needed that hug to forget his stress. He gave me a few pats on the back and moved away from me, asking for us to finish the treatments that required immediate intervention. His tired gaze evaporated and a new one revived. I believe that having a group of foreign faces to attend to gave him some hope that life would not have been stilted in that building.

It was not the pain, nor the wounds encrusted on the skins, nor the pestilence of the bodies, nor the cries, that gave him a particular sparkle. It was absurd to think that someone's pain and suffering could cause joy. Rather, it was his kindness that jumped out of that tall body and dazzled his round eyes, making him fight again to bring comfort to strangers. That was the real effect war had on him. The effect of feeling useful, of feeling needed, of giving help, of overturning that feeling of solidarity that resided within his being, which changed the tiredness.

We finished after two hours. My exhaustion was palpable and the stomach rumblings sounded like grunts invading the inner walls of myself. Dr. Mirren laughed loudly when he saw embarrassment reflected on our faces. His smile showed his even and pearly teeth, up to his gums, and was it like a balm that alleviated all the ills that came attached to the body. The other doctors followed him in this demonstration of empathy, and we united in a burst of pleasant laughter. It was the first time that I had smiled without feeling selfish. Just doing so filled me with joy at something unexpected and natural. It was the first time that my lungs were relieved of anguish and sorrow since I had left Aleppo with Naima, my mother, and Jalila, my sister.

Before night fell in Idlib we had already drunk milk and eaten bread and some fruit. Several children were resting with the other adults, waiting for the next morning to arrive. Although we had no house of our own, the roof that sheltered us was a blessing for that day, along with the clean and dry clothes that kept us warm.

The clinic turned into a quiet place and the cold jealously lurked in the outskirts. The next morning the children had their breakfast. The hot milk smoked in the bowls and, in the cups, the adults' coffee and tea were poured into the throats with melodious gulps. The weary faces of the previous day became more relaxed. Jalila sang to the little ones who had stayed with us: four innocent souls who, like the others who left in search of their families when they arrived in the city, wanted to forget loneliness. The two women and three men who were the last remnants of the caravan were ready, waiting for orders to move.

My mother and I set out to fold the blankets and leave

them on a makeshift wardrobe. My mother broke the silence trying to organize the day. "Don't you think, Samira, that it would be better if you went up to see what they need?" That tone, that was so typical of her, made me look for Dr. Mirren.

I went up to the first floor where we had been received the day before. The doctors made their rounds and cared for the patients. The sound of tweezers falling on metal trays, the smell of disinfectant, and the sound of sterilizing ventilators were part of that common morning that opened up before all of us with responsibilities that couldn't be avoided.

I found Dr. Mirren talking to Laila. Her leg was still oozing, but she looked more rested and calm. The antibiotics and the sedative did their part, now it was up to the man to do the rest. It wouldn't be easy, we all knew that.

I didn't want to interrupt, but he realized that a pair of eyes were looking at him and, with another smile, he got up to say good morning to me.

"Samira, how did you spend the night?", he asked kindly.

"Well, thank you," I replied.

"Have you had coffee yet?"

"No, I would rather that the others had it first."

"Well, I need another cup of coffee, come with me."

We went through the big door where I had entered the day before. The morning sky dawned blue and rays of light seeped through the clouds that crossed it. The grey of the previous day had disappeared. The icy weather continued to lurk, producing harsh noises as it encountered the sand-colored tents just outside the building. A fluffy layer of snow, like a mat receiving our steps to the first tent, welcomed us and Dr. Mirren invited me to sit on a scrawny wooden table next to two folding chairs.

"Sit down, I will come back with the best coffee you have ever tasted," said this man whose height when moving away was comparable to the Buddhas of Bamiyan. Never before I had seen someone so tall.

"All right," I replied and timidly pulled the chair.

I sat down. I remembered that I had to call the number that Dr. Tayyeb had given me in Aleppo. I felt a slight regret. As I waited, my mind again played back images of my past. The ghosts of my childhood and adolescence paraded at ease in front of me, full of smiles. Ever prejudiced to my present, they were having fun at sea and in the mountains, returning to the places where my family had been very happy until not long ago. Like a bird of ill omen, death made itself present as the face of my father. It also did so in the city where he had grown up and lived until a few days ago, filling my only living spaces with crazy dances that moved between fear and tenderness.

Suddenly the growling in my stomach made me realize that I was hungry again and the fragrance of the pasta from the Cantara restaurant that I enjoyed with my father, the filling of the *dolmas*[9] and the softness of the *mujaddara*[10]

---

[9]*Dolmas: Grape leaves stuffed with rice, pine nuts and onions served with lemon.*
[10]*Mujaddara: Dish of lentils and rice served with fried onions and olive oil.*

my mother prepared at home, triggered my appetite making my mouth salivate.

I squeezed my belly with both hands to see if the noises would stop, but it didn't happen, the noises resonated in my belly like the roars of hundreds of lions locked up in a small space.

I saw the doctor approach with two cups of coffee and a tiny pink can. My heart jumped with happiness. I knew that pink can. I had seen it many times on the trips we made with my father outside of Syria. It contained my mother's favorite cookies. I felt safe again when I saw the little box. I was a little girl again.

Dr. Mirren sat down in front of me and put the two cups on the table. The coffee was thick and sweet. It left a trace of velvet on the tongue and on the nose; smells of wood, walnuts and honey. The liquid went down my throat and fell into my stomach warming its numb walls, soothing me. He opened the pink can and offered me what was inside: butter cookies bathed in sugar crystals.

"Go ahead, have as many as you want, they're delicious," he said, "they make me feel closer to home, I keep them like gold." He made the last remark with a hint of sadness, his voice faltering. With our hands wrapped around the coffee cups and feeling the warmth of the liquid inside the ceramic wells, he began to tell me how he had come here, to this forgotten place in the world, where war traps you with its beastly hands, crushing you with its burden of irony.

I learned that Claude Mirren had worked with the

International Physicians Organization for twenty years. His father was of French origin and his mother was Syrian, born in Damascus, raised in the City of Light, of glamour and of the ancient 'Gallic' aristocracy. Both dedicated themselves to medicine. They formed a solid duet where achievements filled the marriage with pride, the same ones that years later would open the doors to their two children, turning the family into an unstoppable quartet. The Mirrens had their father at their head, who practiced pediatrics; their mother, who was a cardiologist; and the sister, who was a gynecologist. Claude was a general surgeon.

The four doctors had taken it as an obligation to help people who could not access first class medical services. The altruism that characterized them made them even more respectable and recognized. The family had their private practice a few blocks from the American Hospital in Paris, on Victor Hugo Boulevard.

When Syria's civil war broke out, Claude Mirren was the first to join in to help. He was a surgeon in Paris at the Hospital de la Pitié-Salpêtriè. Single and with no children, he had completely devoted himself to medicine. He was married to it and although he had had informal affairs, he did not want to be selfish in getting married. His work was demanding, and he felt in his own skin the loneliness he had chosen. He enjoyed it very much. His career had enabled him to travel the world, and his family background gave him the opportunity to chair groups of talented doctors in the organization he represented. During the difficult times in

Israel, Iran, Iraq, Turkey, Ukraine and Latin America, he had saved lives. Thanks to his profession, he moved in influential circles; so, when the International Doctors Organization of France decided to leave for Syria, he was the floor surgeon. Although many on the medical corps had no family ties to Syria, they enlisted because they were convinced that this was their calling and their duty.

A sigh ended the story of his journey, of his experiences in this suffering and bleeding land. His hunched height on the wimpy chair, his thick hands and his coffee breath continued to act charmingly. His life flowed like the waters of a stream that risked drying up; he felt the urgent need to explain himself, to tell his experiences like everyone else. That feeling was something that no one could deny him, so I listened attentively.

His mouth opened wide, letting words out that traveled and suddenly crashed into the morning with the icy wind. He told how one of his colleagues by the name of Suar, the only surgeon in a small town of Zabadani near Damascus, had told him how difficult it was to practice his profession because he was struggling between saving his patients and the welfare of his family, who were also exposed to the danger of death. He had told him that he was reaching a turning point where just seeing children with war wounds was unbearable for him to treat.

"Suar left. Communications are not optimal under these circumstances. I don't know if he managed to go to Germany as he wished. I hope so, I wish to see him again," said Dr. Mirren with painful nostalgia.

An explosion was heard in the distance and made us jump out of our seats. The distant sounds of the bombs made fear soar, making everyone run or look for a safe place. We both finished our break, entered the building and let the day unfold normally despite the events.

At night Jalila, my mother and I slept in one of the tents around the doctors' building with the four children who arrived with us. The tent seemed like a palace to us at the time, the relentless draft of air from outside whipped over our heads, singing a sad tune. The most important thing was that those tents protected us in a symbolic way. I hugged my sister. Her embrace was a double refuge, my body stopped shaking; the warmth and tenderness of her affection gave me security and filled me with strength. I had to go on for her and for my mother. We didn't have anyone else; it was the three of us against the world.

A new day dawned before us. There was something different in the atmosphere. Despite having slept pleasantly I felt restless and an emptiness in my stomach grew. It seemed like a warning. The sun, like a giant sunflower, was rising in the celestial vault; and the snow, in the hands of the children swarming around the clinic, was melting at the same time as mischievous, carefree laughter crossed the blue sky. After providing breakfast to the children and the doctors, we went to work organizing and cleaning. It was the least we could do as a thank you to Dr. Mirren's hospitality.

At noon a Turkish UN convoy made its triumphal entrance. On board, they brought tents, ovens, firewood, clothes, medicines, and blankets. People from the surrounding area ran after the trucks, and the children waved their hands in the wind with smiles that unfolded innocence and hope. In the faces of the doctors, there was a glimpse of relief and satisfaction. After two weeks of waiting, they could finally visit the camp that refugees from other cities such as Madaya, Zabadani, Wadi Barada and Al-Waer, including those from Aleppo, had set up on the banks of the southern road.

At Dr. Mirren's request, my mother stayed at the clinic with Jalila and the three doctors on staff. Along with him, two doctors who came in the convoys that joined the crew and me, headed to the camp without delay. As we approached the southern road, the wind was blowing stronger, the snow was falling harder and far away, a farmhouse with white and blue tents, rose shyly and gloomy in the midst of trees that showed their pointed green branches.

From some of the tents, the smoke rose to the sky in small spheres carrying with them the personal memories of all those who fled from malice and injustice. From other tents, smoke beads flowed like crooked streams signaling that need was pressing and that silence and the frosty weather rocked with them at the edge of the road. At the sound of the engines, a bunch of heads began to appear in disbelief. With a sense of urgency, women, children, and young people began to run beside us; waving their hands as the other inhabitants of Idlib had done when they saw the convoy arrive an hour earlier. When we stopped, hugs and excitement filled the place. Medical care and food distribution tents were erected right away.

Before my eyes, the cruelty of war; children hunched over for lack of vitamin D, young women with the dream of motherhood shattered by miscarriages due to lack of primary care, adults turned into bones and skin, their muscle mass disappeared by feeding only on wheat and peas.

Those were ten hours that tested the energy of our spirit.

On the way to the mobile clinic in the center of Idlib, I borrowed Dr Mirren's cell phone. I dialed the number provided by Dr. Tayyeb before leaving Aleppo. Time went by slowly and with it the cities became empty. I didn't want to be responsible for my mother and sister getting caught in the middle of a crossfire campaign. The uneasiness that I had experienced in the morning hours appeared again, with the same intensity, taking away my peace and increasing my sense of alertness.

The call went through. It rang and rang. No one answered the other side, not even the voicemail was activated. I felt powerless. Dr. Mirren noticed my change of mood, but he didn't ask about it; he just kept staring at the road, where the white frost that accompanied us flooded everything.

After arriving at the clinic, my thoughts continued to hold the long sound that inhabited the telephone line. The intermittent tone was still ringing in my ears, and this sensation depressed me, but on seeing three other UNICEF trucks that brought first aid kits, tents, blankets and especially water and medicines, the discomfort disappeared and a sensation of gratitude filled me. At least for that night.

The head of the UNICEF expedition was waiting for us on

the same corner where Dr. Mirren and I sat down for coffee the day I arrived. That was ago already ago. He introduced himself as Emanuel Goodman. Emanuel already knew Dr. Mirren, from what I could see in their demonstrations of affection. These tall men gave each other a big hug and kissed each other's cheeks with two loud kisses.

Emanuel took the doctor's face in his long hands and said: "Brother, I don't know how you do it. You have to get out of here as soon as possible. Nothing more can be done, you are in danger!" As he walked, he continued: "We have made the most difficult journey of all. We have been shot, bombed and chased. We've been through some suspicious checkpoints, but we're here and it's been worth it. Passing through Damascus and Tartos the roads showed the ravages of war, I would have arrived earlier, but we were stopped for a few hours in Aria."

He gave him a loud pat on the shoulder and, opening the door of his truck, gave him a surprise. A tall, slender woman with blond hair, dressed in a "Prince" T-shirt and cargo pants, came down and hung herself by his neck. The two fused into an infinite and tight embrace; then the three of them.

The spectacular blonde turned out to be Annette, Dr. Mirren's sister, who had just crossed the Antarctic from Norway to be with her brother and take him home to Paris.

As we unloaded the trucks and sorted the articles, I saw Emanuel talking to Raija, a little girl of barely seven who swarmed around the place every day. "I'm glad to see you again," she said. Emanuel drew her to his broad chest, and the little girl's tiny body was lost in the man's arms. He said pulling a handful of milk candies out of his pockets, "here princess, they are your favorites." Raija put her little hand on the American's round face and ran to hide.

Immediately we heard voices and regardless of the time, the neighbors came to help unload the trucks and greet Emanuel and Annette effusively. Apparently, she had met them before. You could tell by the familiarity with which they hugged.

The next afternoon, in the middle of the daily routine of unloading trucks and of medical care, the city came under attack. The hospital shook from its foundations. I was on the first floor caring for some patients; the last thing I could see clearly was a woman with something that looked like a baby in her arms approaching me. Everything else was confusing; the explosions and the screams from outside mixed with those from inside.

The blast that reached the first floor threw me hard on the ground. When I fell, a hot liquid gushed from my eardrums. I was choking on my own air. There was another bang. I heard glass shattering with an amplified sound that made me uneasy. I closed my eyes and then darkness took hold of me.

I don't know how long I remained unconscious. The air inside my chest made my ribs ache and there was a desperate squeal coming from my chest. I felt a hand and a voice speaking to me, but I could not clearly understand his words. Everything was a ball full of unintelligible sounds.

The hand pulled me somewhere; I didn't know exactly where. I could feel his gasping breath and his voice insisting on keeping me awake. He dragged me, I don't know where or how long the distance was. From the position of my head, I knew that he placed my body on a flat surface. All around me was a gray cloud.

I could not quite discern beyond the bright light beaming from his helmet, but I felt his fingers on my side making a hole in the skin of my belly. The warmth of the stream of blood that came out, allowed me to breathe better, the circle of hot air that choked me vanished. Without the intervention of those unknown hands, I would have died immediately, drowned by my own air and my own blood. Of that I was certain.

Part Two

*War is a massacre between people
who do not know each other, for the benefit of
people who do know each other but who do not
massacre each other.*
Paul Valéry *(1871-1945)*

Al-Ramtha, Amman and Zaatari

When I opened my eyes at Al-Ramtha Hospital in northern Jordan, I saw his face. I didn't recognize him. In reality, I didn't remember anything before my arrival at the hospital. I knew my name because I had my passport with me, hanging around my neck when I arrived in Jordan, and because the doctors kept repeating it constantly when they were treating me. Most of the days I spent sunk in persistent drowsiness and headaches. I was plagued by an extreme sensitivity to light and vomiting. But when Ahmed Bakri appeared before me, with his wide torso, soft gaze and dark skin, it enveloped me in such a way that my reality, and the terrible things in it, took a different course and I only clung to a strange magic that emanated from him. I could never put into words the effect he had on me. It was something I felt, and it stayed with me for the rest of my life.

"My name is Ahmed Bakri, I'm a freelance reporter, do you remember anything about what happened at the medical center? You're the only survivor."

His introduction and his questions were in that order. I didn't understand anything. Everything was confusing; I looked at him shocked, frowning. I tried to get out of bed, but I got dizzy and I begged him: "Get me out of here, I want to go home."

During my month of stay in the hospital, I had intermittent memories in my dreams along with severe migraines. Figures from the past whom I should have known appeared in some of them; from others, there were visions where my inner self listened to its own footsteps and its agitated breathing in ravaged and cold roadways.

A handful of memories, like flashes, showed smiling faces in front of a train. In others, I was having ice cream or I was riding a bicycle surrounded by green, flat vegetation, with leafy trees that gave off the scents of spring. I wasn't sure if I had a family, no one had visited me during my stay in Al-Ramtha. My head had misplaced both recent and distant memories. It was a box full of particles floating incoherently; where the origins of many things unable to replicate themselves again.

The reporter's warm embrace comforted me. Ahmed stroked my hair and asked me to remain silent by placing his ring finger on my lips. Gently, he accommodated the pillows and commented with a tired voice, "The city, Idlib, was besieged by the rebels. Also, those of the Al-Nusra Front are surrounding it along with infiltrators of Daesh. There is disarray and chaos just as there is in Aleppo. The medical center where you were found is in ruins; doctors and patients dead. I thought you could help me, but I see it is you who needs my help."

I didn't say anything. I pulled the bed sheets against my chest. Ahmed asked me to rest; said that he would take care of me. Trapped in the hospital, I sank into the softness of the pillows. I closed my eyes again, accompanied by a freelance journalist of whom I knew absolutely nothing and who had, inadvertently, promised to take care of me.

Ahmed traveled from Idlib through all the roads to get to me, because I was the only survivor of the insurgents' attack on the medical center. The international medical community demanded justice, as did the French government. Asking here and there, he learned that there was only one person still alive who, he thought, would provide him details of the explosion. Otherwise, he could report about the rubble without witnesses.

Ahmed took me out of the hospital the day after his visit. During the trip it confused and irritated me that I was unable to give him exact details of what had happened in Idlib. Now I was traveling to Amman with a stranger and a backpack full of donated clothes. We were on Route 10 from Ramtha to Irbid. Thirty-eight minutes of silence until we reached the hotel where Ahmed had booked his stay.

The Al-Joude Hotel was not luxurious, but it was what Ahmed could afford. The sand-colored building was surrounded by palm trees and rose bushes. In front of the main entrance there was a parking lot and, through it, a beautiful rest area where the water from the fountain splashed in cheerful, uniform streams. We stayed in room 307 which looked quite clean; the queen bed, the magenta color on the wall and the cream-colored curtains matched harmoniously. There was an armchair. There were photographs and a laptop computer on the night table.

Ahmed, seeing that the bed was the center of my attention,

mentioned that he would settle on the floor; that he was used to the floor and, pointed out, that he would go out to buy something to eat; because the food at the hotel was not appetizing.

"Samira, relax and take a shower. Rest will do you good."

"Thank you, it sounds tempting. Hospitals aren't comfortable. I say that from experience."

Silence.

As soon as Ahmed left, I took off my shoes and fell asleep in a matter of seconds, lulled by the streams of water from the water fountain.

Thirsty, I woke up to the sound of the door. I saw Ahmed enter with a bag full of bread, olives and soft drinks. I got out of bed and fixed my hair, which looked like the branches of a cedar tree, tying it in a ponytail. I sat on the sofa and the smell of the bread, which Ahmed placed on the corner table, hit my nose. It was the smell of an ancestral legacy traveling through the nostrils. I took a deep breath trying not to let go of the aroma that intoxicated my senses in a way that made me happy. I took a piece and dipped it in the spiced oil that bathed the olives. I felt a stab in my chest and one of my mental gaps opened as ripe dates open, giving way to a subtle voice that had no name, but which spoke of olives, their tender flesh and the delight of dipping freshly baked bread in oil. I shuddered, and from one moment to the next, I traversed from happiness to tears. I apologized to Ahmed, and he hugged me, consoling me with a tender phrase that made me feel a little better.

"Everything will be fine, we are the children of a land that has lived in radiance and penumbra. We are like the Phoenix. Allah does not abandon his children, we will know how to sail the seas of bitterness or sadness. We will win, we will win, you will see."

"Thank you, Ahmed. I have no way to repay you for what you do for me."

We hugged, and he wiped my tears with the red plaid scarf that covered his neck.

The next morning, after a bath, a cup of sage tea and a few plates of fried eggplant, falafel and yogurt at the hotel cafeteria, we went to Amman. Ahmed was going take me to the UNHCR offices to register and apply for asylum services, which I was hoping would be temporary. Ahmed treated the subject very carefully, and I processed it with fear and anxiety. I had no other way out; I had to begin somewhere, and this seemed most appropriate based on my condition and to his way of life. He was an independent reporter and had to follow his call. I was just a coincidence and I had to learn to survive by myself. He was already doing enough.

I had the compelling need to get out of that land and everything that surrounded it, to get beyond its borders, probably as an illusion that gave me some security or it was possibly the invisible imprint of the sorrows that I could not remember.

The only thing that was truly mine now was my passport, from which I never for an instant let out of my sight. I wore it around my neck inside my dress just like I did when they found me and when I arrived at the hospital.

We arrived in Amman around half past ten in the morning. The journey was comfortable despite the fact that the vehicle Ahmed drove (a very old cream-colored Mercedes Benz that emitted dreadful noises) seemed, at every gear change, as if it was going to break down on the road. It took us almost an hour and a half to cover sixty-seven kilometers from the Al-Joude Hotel to the block before where the UNHCR building stood on Wasfi Al-Tal Street. During the journey the conversation did not flow as it would under normal circumstances, but the ride went smoothly, with a few comments from Ahmed about Irbid and its popularity as the second most populous city in the Kingdom of Jordan; its universities, its people and the landscapes that attracted tourists from all over the world.

Ahmed was patient and kind. At no time did he force me to reveal my feelings, which were confused at that time. Rather, he let me relax and carry out my communion with the horizon, while his soft, mystical gaze was lost in the countryside. Upon entering the city of Amman, the panorama changed to that of a modern, liberal city. In the parking lot we called the number that Ahmed registered on his cell phone when he left the hotel in Irbid, but it was Friday and the customer service offices were only open through Thursday. We had to change our immediate plans.

"Well," I said, "if we must wait, then we don't have a choice." But I wasn't convinced, I was very scared, and everything around me made me uncomfortable.

"Yes, you're right," said Ahmed smiling, "the waiting is quite boring at times, would you like to tour the city?"

There wasn't much to do at the moment, the best thing was to relax. Ahmed had the ability to take me to another world. To a space where my fears didn't exist. Where loneliness was more bearable, and pivotal moments evaporated giving way to tranquility. Then, agreeing with him, we got out of the car and started to walk. Ahmed didn't know the whole city either. In those war years, he had only gone back and forth to the border, to hospitals and to the offices of the independent television station where he sold his articles. The weather did not prevent us from enjoying the simple things, such as people, who, despite the fact that it was a day of "observance" -as Ahmed explained - walked, wrapped in big coats, with their shopping; or tourists, owners of other languages that mixed with Arabic. As we walked the streets, we coexisted in silence with the winter nature of Amman which, beautiful, stood upon seven mountains. We circled part of the city until we reached Rainbow Street, a long street with its shops and stairs covered by the snow.

The open cafés and restaurants invited us to enjoy a life that continued to develop between the art and culture of those who inhabited it and those of us who passed through it. Ahmed had heard wonders about the Souk Jara bazaar and we decided to pay it a visit. Upon arrival, its long and colorful corridors invited visitors to photograph themselves and purchase extraordinary items such as blown glass crafts, jewelry, leather pieces, and perfumes.

In only a few meters, I was able to enjoy the things that were locked in a place inside my mind without a consistent form. We laughed in front of the merchants who were watching us, accompanied by the smoke from the *shishas*[11]. The people who walked through those places, covered in embroidery, were the owners of friendly faces. Inside the small bazaars, we were allowed to see anything we liked without being pressured to buy anything. We even found Iraqi bills, with the face of Saddam Hussein, which Ahmed did not hesitate to buy in order to increase the scrawny collection he treasured in his wallet.

By mid-morning, we stopped for lunch at Al-Quds, an old restaurant where we were served a delicious *mansaf*[12] made of saffron rice and lamb with yogurt sauce. At times I let fear overtake me, but I decided to keep the nervousness of my condition within me and trust that journalist. Something inside told me that everything would be fine if I stayed by his side.

At coffee time Ahmed made several calls, writing down phone numbers on a paper napkin. While he was talking, I sipped my coffee giving myself to the task of observing him. I could see that on his face the change of the seasons had made its mark, but that the war had not completely robbed him of his generosity. After a while, Ahmed smiled broadly showing his white teeth. He had been able to locate his friend Abba who worked for a local newspaper and who,

---

[11]*Shisha: A type of molasses and vegetable glycerin based tobacco that is smoked with a device called hookah.*

[12]*Mansaf:Plato de origen beduino que es propio de la cocina Jordana y Turca a base de cordero, arroz y yogur.*

years earlier, had become a legal citizen of Jordan. He would house us for the remainder of the weekend until we could return to the refugee offices first thing Sunday morning. Ahmed put away his cell phone telling me that we were lucky: Abba would lend us his studio for the rest of the weekend since he had to work overtime at the newspaper. He wouldn't be back until Sunday afternoon. The studio wasn't far; it was number 123 Al-Khattab Street past Book@ cafe. Ahmed took my right hand joyfully, squeezing it gently, and I was pleased. I was pleased to feel the touch of his skin. His company was a feast in my new life full of darkness.

After the good news about the accommodations, we carried on with our coffee and our conversation. He told me more about things I couldn't remember. About everything that happens when you feel trapped in a country you no longer recognize, or a country you don't belong to. For Ahmed, Syria and Jordan were present in his heart and in his mind, the same as Turkey and Lebanon. Each of these lands with their streams, rivers, trees, with their people and architecture, had been welcomed by him and, in each one, their own beauty and vileness had left him with as many memories as scars.

Every time he spoke, I somehow processed his feelings as mine, keeping them in a part of my heart. I was attracted to him. I didn't know exactly what was happening to me or why, but I didn't fight the affection that slipped through me. We asked for another coffee and then it occurred to me to ask, "How is it that you, being a Syrian, can move about on Jordanian soil?" After taking a deep breath, he replied that he was traveling light, with a legal Jordanian passport, acquired on the black market in Lebanon. A long story that began at the beginning of the war when it was still possible to travel between borders without any problem. Knowing that this confrontation with the Syrian regime would not be resolved overnight, he traveled to Lebanon in search of fake documents to mobilize in case of emergency. He used most of his savings and a whole new world opened up before his eyes. He discovered that people are forced to do jobs that are not entirely honest.

Then the stories take a different course and their threads end in a web that is very difficult to disentangle. He said this because parallel to the news of what was happening in Syria, he had discovered organ trafficking. Remains of people without their organs had been found. They didn't even bother to dig a pit; they let them bleed to death. It was something that happened inside and outside Syria, as the refugees were victims of the system. Ahmed said all this with a tone of anger and frustration. He swallowed the bitter gulp of the conversation with a sip of coffee steaming up from the small golden-edged cup, while I imagined those open bodies clutching the hanging guts, or the faces with only two holes filled with pus from the lack of their eyes, or the backs open with two slits to remove their kidneys.

The sound of a plate falling to the ground away from our table made me come back to reality and listen carefully to what Ahmed was saying.

His way of moving his hands when speaking, his pupils changing color according to his emotions, his deep, firm voice with tones of tenderness attracted me to the conversation even more. There was a moment when Ahmed stared at me, I had the feeling that he would kiss me, but he didn't, and he continued with the conversation.

"This wears me out like the war itself," he said, "when the need is pressing everything has a price." He accompanied his thought with a gesture of disgust which included dilated pupils that made his eyes darker, and he threw his back on the chair, nailing his fingertips to the surface of the table. To my surprise, I was taking in the grim conversation that always ends up in a black hole, according to what my reporter to the rescue had told me so far. Apparently, he was determined not only to make known the misfortunes of the civil war but also all the consequences that it caused by not seeing peace. As I listened to him, a shiver ran down my back, raising all the hairs on my body. A slight fear took hold of all my muscles. A thousand random questions crossed my mind as he stared at me, with those chocolate-colored eyes, trying to guess my next question or my next move. I had no words to express what I was feeling because I didn't know exactly what it was. I put my left hand on his, to reassure him and myself as well. Then I said, "The portrait of an embodied verb, that's what we are."

We took a break, deep in our thoughts looking out onto the street, me with my hand on his left hand, focusing on the dim lights of the streetlights of that neighborhood that could be seen behind the windows of the family restaurant. We finished the coffee with short sips. Evening fell, and the cold became more pronounced. Ahmed asked if I was ready to go looking for his friend's studio where we would spend the night. I nodded. He paid the check, and we headed towards Al-Khattab Street with our hands in our pockets, him in his blue jeans and I in my imitation leather coat, that had been given in the hospital.

Soon we were at the edge of the street where the windows on the first floor were white over the guava-colored wall. We climbed a narrow staircase of large mosaics in matching colors. Arriving at the door of the studio, we set out to keep the bad thoughts away. Ahmed found the key in a slot made on purpose in the corner of the window. When he put it in the door plate, he turned and in a conciliatory tone said to me, "Let's make a deal, Samira. As long as we are together and as long as we are under this roof, let's try to forget what is going on outside." I smiled and reaffirmed my intention to put aside the misfortunes that hung from us, caressing one of his cheeks with the back of my hand.

Once inside, we felt safe in a way. Backpacks and shoes were left on one side of the door. We dropped onto the narrow bed stuck to one of the internal windows overlooking a tiny courtyard decorated only by a table and two chairs. "Well, well, your friend Abba, for a bachelor, has good taste," I said in a mocking tone, and we restarted the conversation focusing on Sunday's activities when we would visit UNHCR.

I don't know when tiredness defeated us and forced us to

close our eyes. One movement led to another and we gave way, unintentionally, to a casual intimacy without haste, a selfish intimacy. We both wanted company. We wanted to leave behind the sorrows, the losses and the uncertainty; and it was logical that being alone, in such a reduced space, our bodies would look for each other among the cream colors of the shade hanging from the ceiling; of the starched white sheets that produced a musical rustle laying on them, and of the guava walls that transported us to something similar to happiness.

Since it was already nighttime, I turned on the small copper lamp that was on the table next to the bed. Its round shape with stars gave the room a warmer atmosphere, inviting calm and seduction to do their work. Ahmed took my hand, led it to his mouth and kissed it tenderly. I accommodated myself by his side and let the curly-haired mane with its bluish black drop freely on his chest. "I'm scared," I whispered.

Ahmed's skin smelled of sweet sweat and tobacco. Not a grotesque smell, rather of mansaf, of coffee and that air that permeates the urgent races against time. We caressed each other without distrust, lavishing each other with hugs, intensifying them as desire took care of us. Slowly he removed my clothes. I allowed his long fingers and firm touch to rouse my libido with prolonged and delicate caresses. In a bold moment, he mounted me and explored my intimacy with rotating motions. He kissed my belly, my flat breasts, my neck, and sank into my hair as his member gently and then quickly entered me. I enjoyed discovering sex with my kind and melancholic man. I was enjoying the fluttering breath and the intermittent moans coming from our throats. I felt his fingers in my hair, his mouth carried the flavor of a man who has fought a thousand battles, owner of a thousand lives that stuck to the skin in a solid and impulsive way. I closed my eyes for an endless time, then I felt a discharge inside me that brought my body to shudder together with his. I was embarrassed by the desire. Ahmed with his natural sweetness smiled and kissed me lightly, whispering in my ear that being with me was a gift. We made love, smiled and cried. We ended our feat with a long kiss. In the arms of that kind stranger, I spent a day and a whole night. We both abandoned ourselves to our pleasure and to our primitive desires to become one. We began to speak to each other with our lips; words were superfluous. We invented a language where the corners of our mouths traveled the eternal path of pleasure. Ahmed taught me to find pleasure as I roamed his body. We learned to love each other because we spoke to our souls with respect. After that moment there was nothing but us and our hearts healing by new emotions. Our silhouettes articulated the perpetual and the infinite of nudity. Sex allowed us to escape from the logical side of our consciousness.

The next morning when I woke up, breakfast was on the tiny island that separated the space between the bed and the bathroom. That reduced space has been one of the fondest memories I would carry with me in the next phase of my life. Ahmed's look captivated me; he seemed taller and stronger on the other side of the room dressed only in his pants. He crossed the island and lifted me by putting his hands on my arms. I was holding the sheet because the embarrassment of seeing myself naked in broad daylight it made me uncomfortable. But just as he taught me pleasure, he also taught me that there was nothing wrong with my nudity, that my nakedness was perfect, desirable, and respectable.

He kissed me on the forehead, then on the cheeks and took me by the hand to the kitchen counter for breakfast. I got rid of the sheets that kept on emitting their musical noises until they fell to the floor. We walked hand in hand and I let myself be pampered by receiving his hot and foamy coffee. Full of peace, I ate what he had prepared. It was Saturday, there was no rush to go anywhere, all we needed was inside those four walls.

On Sunday, before leaving Abba's small studio, we made the bed, washed the dishes and prepared to go to the UNHCR office. Ahmed left a note for his friend and took some dinars out of his wallet, folded them in half and placed them under the salt shaker. I walked the narrow space for the last time with that chill I had felt on Friday afternoon as we drank coffee at Al-Quds. I thought it was the feeling of setting aside significant moments that I was experiencing after my departure from the hospital, in addition to the loss of memory and the expectation of my visit to the refugee office. The truth is that the shudder escalated with the passing of minutes. We closed Abba's studio and deposited the key in the same place where we found it. Then we disappeared again among the other cars and the streets.

Upon reaching Wasfi Al-Tal Street, the UNHCR building rose high like a crystal castle where the sunlight and the celestial clouds of that Sunday were reflected. Inside, long corridors led visitors to the various offices. Once inside, we were taken to a large room where hundreds of families waited to be received. Ahmed took a number from a machine indicating the location on the waiting list. One of the officials greeted us with a smile welcoming us, giving me a folder to be filled with my personal details. We sat next to each other, waiting for the cases to be processed until we were called. The sadness of not knowing who I was stirred inside me. Ahmed sensed my nervousness and squeezed my hand. Silently he filled out my form using the information in my passport.

"Ahmed, can I ask about my family here?"

"I don't know Samira, there are too many displaced people to locate. But if we ask, they'll surely give us a clue, there are lists and every week someone arrives here. If you have a family, they'll show up. However, don't get your hopes up, remember that you were the only survivor in the clinic; they are still digging up bodies and, without a memory of your own, it will be almost impossible to know."

I didn't ask any more questions, I just tried not to cry. The wait was long, too long for my preference. When I arrived at the window, they processed my application automatically, without a smile, without a look of sympathy. The tapping of the seal with which they authenticated my documents sounded like a symphony hammering inside my head. "Here you go, you can go to Zaatari's shelter today. You have a monthly allowance and will share a tent with four women. Your appointment for medical examination is ready for the following week; you have to go to the Italian hospital located in district D5 in Zaatari. We will put out an alert to see if anyone in your family is in Amman or if they are in the camp."

The face furrowed with a few wrinkles, the black eyes hidden behind large plastic-rimmed glasses and a serious voice, dismissed me with a "have a good day" and calling the next number indicated by the automatic sign on his window.

We left the place in silence. We walked back to the block where Ahmed's car was and we headed to the outskirts of Amman. Ahmed commented that Zaatari had become a sort of citadel, with shops and bakeries, where the streets had been named and where both women and men got up to go to work. He tried to make the farewell less hard by talking in a humorous tone about the camp, mentioning the good things, the group work and the short time I would be there. He couldn't take care of me. I knew then that I had to learn to live with my own ghosts myself. It hurt, but that was my reality and he was aware of the same.

We were only a few minutes away from Zaatari; we traveled seventy-six kilometers to Mafraq. While Ahmed spoke, I saw on one side of the road the camp, the second largest in the Middle East, opening up like a fan across a desert bordering Syria only twelve kilometers away. My heart beat rapidly and my mouth felt dry. Before my eyes, everything looked as pure as it was brutal.

When the car stopped in front of the big white tent with blue letters, I felt my extremities cramping. My knees became stiff and my feet icy. The door handle was glued to my hand. I don't know when Ahmed got off, but suddenly I saw him standing in front of the car. I got out and went to the tent where the security guards drank hot tea and watched television. Ahmed looked at me and I looked back. I held his hand waiting for him to ask me to leave with him. I was waiting for something that wasn't going to happen. I inhaled to gain strength and approached one of the guards.

I held my tears out of mere pride. I showed the UNHCR letter to a man with a prominent belly holding the remote control of the television. He inspected my documents. He looked at me and, giving me a map and the meal schedule, told me to go to the other side of the tent, opening it with disdain. The snow extended endlessly on the way and was surrounding the weak tents and containers that served as homes. In small mounds, the snow seemed to climb to devour them completely. Children ran playing hide-and-seek. A boy walked with difficulty, covering his feet with pieces of plastic, dragging a bucket of water. There were men smoking cigarettes, women shaking blankets, and suddenly I was there, facing an uncertain future.

Leaving the registration tent, Ahmed shouted: "I will not leave you in this hell Samira, I promise to come back for you." I ran into his arms and asked him to keep his promise.

"Don't leave me, I won't be able to resist this life that reflects sadness."

"I will return. Trust me, Samira."

His body, which gave off a comfortable warmth, let go of me and quickly got into his car and disappeared. With a knot in my chest, I walked towards the tent they had designated for me, the TW68. Arriving at the end of district D7, I found my dwelling. It was the same as the others, white with blue letters, located solitarily in a kind of *cul de sac*[13]. Two women cleaning the surroundings invited me in, welcoming me as if I were part of their clan, as if they had known me all their lives.

The TW68 tent was inhabited by four women, some widows and others single; I would be the fifth. The tent looked very clean and the items in it well arranged. The blankets folded in four on the mattresses. Between each of them, three-level plastic drawers. In the center, a gas oven on a red carpet and an old straw broom. The floor of the tent was raised on a wooden frame that prevented rain or snow from wetting its interior. The scent of sage dominated the atmosphere. I left my backpack and took off my shoes sitting in front of the oven to warm up. Two women served me tea and introduced themselves. Hanan and Malak were sisters who had fled Hama two years earlier. They told me about Shaimae and Cedra, who were widows. The war had killed their families and at that time they were in the city working

---

[13]*Cul de Sac: French term used to designate a road without exist.*

in cleaning services. They would arrive in the afternoon on the motorway 10 that passed by the camp. People who left Zaatari had a permit with which they could move freely in the nearby areas, could not work, but the two of them still managed to do so.

After a few minutes, a vehicle was heard and two men arrived with a mattress, two blankets and a pillow that they had brought from the storage room. I put my mattress down and went to bed, I stayed there until the next day. Shaimae and Cedra had to work in the city at their cleaning jobs. Although they didn't have a work permit, they had to support themselves, and the monthly amount they received as aid was not enough. They wanted to raise money to start a business later. Hanan and Malak were lining up in the bathrooms to wash up because they were going to sell their embroidered handkerchiefs at a vintage business in downtown Amman. The owner bought four boxes of twelve handkerchiefs from them each month. They were paid enough, although not as much as the business owner earned from the sale.

As soon as the women left, I was relieved. I didn't want to talk or listen to anyone's hardships. I wanted to close my eyes and forget myself in a long dream. However, I forced myself to go on a tour of the camp. I got to know the bathrooms, the storerooms, the shops that had been set up, the bakery and some of the recreation centers that the French and Spanish governments had set up so that the children wouldn't be on the streets all day. I somehow wanted to start getting used to the idea that my reality was that: a refugee camp divided into districts, with hospitals, public kitchens, businesses and schools, where the main streets were Al-Yasmine and Ring Street. I had to start assimilating to it for my own good, and try to accommodate my present within those five square kilometers of pressed earth that Ahmed had described to me on the way here.

I saw that the camp was a small town where hope took shelter in the corners. In every face I saw, I could feel that every Syrian participated in the reconstructing of his own life working for the welfare of Zaatari. That was his home, a piece of his country in ruins. Everything around Zaatari was filling up with its customs, and those of us who inhabited it were responsible for it. Along the way, I saw vegetable shops, bicycle shops, bridal gowns, toys, and two large supermarkets. My eyes could not believe that there were private chains in a refugee camp. The streets were filled with the footsteps of countless refugees who greeted the passers-by with affable glances.

I stopped in District 8 and saw a hairdresser and a pizzeria. To my left, a cell phone store stood up airy and busy. I figured that in time I could do something if I put my mind to it. I also thought that in Zaatari, the concept of a refugee camp changed completely to that of a city of twelve districts full of colors and textures. As I walked the narrow streets filled with snow and mud, I wondered if I would ever be normal again, if my lost memory would find its way back to that present that was a bundle of fears. Upon arriving at the communal baths, I saw many mothers bathing their daughters, and daughters scrubbing the bodies bruised by the cold of their brothers and sisters. I made my way through them to a shower where the soap scum drained through a tiny hole and I felt like taking a bath. I undressed and felt the icy wind sticking to my body. When I opened the shower and the water poured down on me, the combination of the wind and the liquid made me shiver at first contact. I realized that I had neither soap or shampoo; the lady who was bathing her daughter offered me, with unusual promptness, a used piece.

I hastened to wash and the smell of cleanliness flooded my nose. In the same way that I was given soap, another woman offered me a towel. So I was able to see that even though I was alone, there was always someone to take care of me.

On my way back to the tent, I lay on the mattress again, and the heat emitted by the portable oven enveloped me while falling asleep. I woke up when the wind began to beat the tents, making them dance harshly. The noise that came with it charged at us from the outside. It was like hearing a lion's roar. I stuck my head out of the tent; the wind wrung the skin of my face again. I looked up at the sky as if waiting for an answer, then the snow started to fall hard on the camp invading us for the next three days. Sunken in resignation and darkness, Hanan, Malak, Shaimae, Cedra and I lay on the mattresses. Zaatari was in complete silence, making time pass slowly. From time to time there were slight whispers as we went to the baths. Especially the wailing of the children who felt the cold in their buttocks as they sat on the toilets. It was uncomfortable to leave the tent and walk through some streets to the public restrooms, even more so at night. The snow was eating off part of our feet and legs with its crystalline teeth, making the skin bleed. Most of the time we held as much as we could the urge to go to the toilet, especially because in the tent the women had told me that several rapes and disappearances of women and girls had been reported.

As developed as Zaatari was, it was still a place with great needs. Not all families were able to get used to or progress within the existing limitations. While it was true that the camp had made great progress, it was also true that misery haunted the streets every day, and with it, misdeeds also invaded the streets. I had heard from my neighbors Omar and Hilal, that it was better to have died in Syria than to feel imprisoned in a Hashemite camp. They were both elderly and perhaps felt they had no purpose. Hilal was seventy-two years old and was going blind.

Wrapped in my blankets I thought a lot about Ahmed. I didn't know when I would see him again, so I decided to sail in nostalgia, remembering the broadness of his chest and the warmth of his kisses. I wasn't in the mood for anything else. On the fourth day, the sky was drawn in mauve colors and the sun began to display its golden arms. Hanan and Malak cleared the entrance with shovels while Shaimae and Cedra put on their rubber boots and bundled up to go to work. The men smoked, and others carried pieces of plastic on their bicycles to patch up the damage to their homes.

People came and went. Women carried their sick children tied to their chests with colorful shawls that came out as part of the hijab, hanging blankets or wet clothes on makeshift clotheslines. Despite the freezing and harsh weather, the community continued its work: they repaired wheelchairs, made desks for the schools, and school uniforms were transported swiftly on their heads. Other residents carried chunks of firewood to heat the tents, and towards the exit, there were those who walked to the highway to go to their poorly paid jobs. Hanan asked me to help her clear the snow from the entrance; I reluctantly followed her.

"Our life is very difficult, Samira," she said, breaking the silence. "We were teachers in Hama; we had a father and a mother. We knew everyone in our city, and we were happy. We have to learn to survive, to get along with ourselves and the world."

"Hanan, you have memories, I have nothing. I will do my best to get up and help." That's all I said, we shook our clothes out and went back into the tent.

Malak was already embroidering the new handkerchiefs that they would sell the following month. Hanan joined in by threading colorful silk threads into the fine needles. I threw myself back on the mattress and imagined living in the countryside where snow was supplanted by golden desert sand and the white tents with blue letters, by houses with winter vegetation hanging from the windows. I dreamt of a school where Hanan and Malak taught and with a thousand smiles mingling with the colors of the history and geography book covers.

A week had passed since I had arrived in Zaatari. The routine in which I lived was a way of dying. I wanted to change my attitude, but everything around me was sad, it hurt me. I looked at myself in the mirror that Malak had on her plastic drawer chest, I adjusted my hijab, I put on a little of Hanan's blush and I left the tent heading to District 5 where I had my doctor's appointment at the hospital. Although the snowstorm had calmed down, the force of the wind prevented me from walking faster. Since I was on time, I took the opportunity to take a detour to the communal bathroom. As I turned the corner of the building, I heard screams, I ran and I saw a robust man drag a girl out of the bathroom. I screamed at the top of my lungs, and I couldn't believe that nobody was coming to help. I kept screaming; the man let go of the girl, who ran disappearing into the streets. Then he approached me with a firm step, pointing a gun at me.

"Shut up, bitch. Shut up, or I'll blow your brains out."

I obeyed and that's when I felt a pinch in the neck; my vision became cloudy. I heard gunshots and the images of bodies running with sticks faded. Then I saw no more.

Towards Mosul

I woke up in a vehicle in where I was traveling with more people. I felt their agitated breathing; and once again their groaning and crying. The pinch had left me quite stunned, but I struggled and slowly got up using my hips and buttocks as support until I had my back in a more comfortable position. I was barefoot and the hood I wore, along with the confined space, caused me anguish. I began to scream in despair: "Get me out of here! Where am I? What do you want from me?" I repeated it several times. A woman's voice asked me, in between sobs, not to make things worse, to calm down, that there was nothing to do, that we were captives.

What was waiting for me? I asked myself, again and again, as my body trembled. Hours later we heard that the transport where they had us made a stop, then another and another. Then the doors opened. I am sure more cars were parked near the truck because several doors opened at once and I heard orders in Arabic as well as in English. I tried to grasp the conversations, but the sentences were short and the cold on my legs and breasts didn't help much. The only thing I got at the end was the name of a city: Mosul.

"I think they're taking us to Mosul," I said to the person next to me, but I didn't get a response, just the same whimpers I'd heard during the trip. They shoved us into another vehicle, calling us bitches, touching our breasts and making obscene gestures on our necks while slapping us on the back and on the head so that we would go up in a hurry. My dignity was trampled on by a group of men who didn't mind treating us worse than animals. We walked as fast as we could, falling on top of each other. I tried to calm down, however, inside the vehicle, the musty air of the truck became denser and the mixing smells were vomit-inducing.

When we arrived at our destination, one of the men outside demanded silence and that the lights and engines of the vehicles that were coming with us to be turned off. When they opened the door of the truck, they lined us up and untied our feet emphasizing that we should be silent, or they would blow our heads off with one shot. We walked in a sepulchral silence, in single file, feeling the cement scratching under our bare feet. Again we heard the male voices greeting each other; there were also female voices. Then they began to untie our wrists and they removed our hoods.

The light of some big lanterns crashed in front of my eyes, I covered my face and waited a few seconds to open them slowly. I began to see the faces of women and girls on my left. I saw two young blondes with fine features and big blue eyes embrace each other. Their wrists were purple from the ties; they were fourteen years old at most. Other women had curly hair, like a short afro, and they had yellow almond eyes. Their toasted skins shone despite the hustle and bustle to which they had been exposed. They were of medium height, perhaps the same size as me, and possibly my age: twenty-four years old. There were girls of nine or ten years old, their trembling bodies clinging to the skirts of the four older women. Finally, I saw a woman who looked pregnant, her face was delicate, sprinkled with thin freckles, of prominent cheekbones, a wide nose, and red hair; her lips were fleshy and chapped. Her hands embraced the belly with attachment. That motherly embrace would never reach her son. He would not grow up under the protection of that red-haired woman. He would be sold.

I saw more women. They all looked down at the ground, except me. Somehow, I wanted to know who the people around me were, what they were like. I tried to find out where they came from by their skin and their eyes and guess who my executioner would be.

"Damn it bitch! Look down, the caliph is about to arrive," said the smelly, cracked-faced man.

I felt a slap in my face, which made my blood boil. I was frightened and angry at the same time. I looked again into the eyes of the man of sour and haughty character, I held his gaze in defiance of his orders for the second time. Then he grabbed my chin and shouted, looking at me furiously.

"You have to lower your head out of respect for our *Wali*[14], do you understand? Do you all understand?" Without further delay, he added: "This is for all! The girls and young virgins will be divided into groups; the others will serve the soldiers. Those who convert to Islam will be the mothers

---

[14]*Wali: its meaning in Arabic is "he who governs all".*

of our children, the future heroes of the cause with all the honors this deserves. Those who do not will suffer the punishment of their own arrogance and disobedience; they will have a short time to think about it." When he finished speaking, he squeezed my face harder. I thought his hands would shatter my chin, they trembled, and his lower lip also trembled with anger. The famous caliph made his triumphal entrance. He was young, not more than thirty-five years old; muscular, tall, with an athletic body and a deep gaze. He walked erect, proud, with his arms behind his back, his firm combatant-like stride made him look like a prince. A prince of evil.

In his black eyes, I could see that he was the Devil on Earth. He was dressed in black from head to toe. All around, everyone lowered their heads as he passed and the women beside him emitted a diabolical guttural chanting of praise to that man, capable of terrorizing families by taking their daughters and wives to convert them under the horror of intimidation and threats. His big mouth, with prominent lips, was the cause of all alarm; the words that came out of it were a cause for fright.

I forgot the warning and challenged him shouting as he passed in front of me after checking hands and teeth of the women to my right, and weighing their breasts using his hands as a bowl as if he were going to buy tomatoes or melons. He checked the girls' ears, their hair, and armpits. The poor girls looked at him frightened; they went through that routine inspection losing a little piece of their dignity.

"You have no right over me or any people, let us go free," I shouted.

This last sentence echoed throughout that courtyard full of strangers. A shovel hit my calves and knocked me to my knees. There was a distempering cry which came out from the throats of those who were in the same situation. Then another shovel blow left me lying face down. I grunted in one. The caliph did not bother to speak to me; he squatted in front of me in defiance, he stared at me with his black eyes and snapped his fingers, ordering the big foul-smelling man to do something, which I interpreted as a scathing punishment.

The women and girls were quickly separated into two groups and taken away, leaving me alone in the courtyard. I thought they would kill me, that I would die from a shot in the head for not controlling myself and defying those who had us under their power. But no, they didn't shoot me. In the midst of my worries, the flesh on my back was torn by lashings. The first one was by surprise, the sound of the whip cut the air and the pain it caused a piercing pain. I counted one, two, three, four, five, and with each one I begged heaven for an end to my ordeal, the blood from my back running hot and falling on the pavement. With the last lashing, I peed myself, and shame consumed me when I saw the shadow of a black tunic over me. A plump face with slanted eyes smiled.

Lying in the middle of helplessness in that rugged and ghostly courtyard, my spirit took flight... I flew far away...

I flew to Irbid where I ate bread dipped in oil with spices, where the voice of an unnamed child spoke to me... I flew to Ahmed's arms, to his eyes framed by thick eyelashes and eyebrows, I flew to Amman where I walked through the Souk Jara bazaar and where there was a table painted with a round lamp carved with stars, the one that once invoked a sense of calm.

I opened my eyes when I heard female voices. I saw the violet and gold colors of dawn and two light-eyed women came for me, helping me to stand up. One of them whispered, " What you did wasn't a good idea. Come, lean on us, everything is going to be fine." The other wrapped me in a blanket that covered my naked and bloody flesh.

Stunned by the lashes I stayed in a corner with the burning in my back and I saw how the young women who said they were virgins were taken to a special room where they were washed and tidied up to be offered for sale. The same was done with the girls. My turn came: they washed me, dressed me and then took me to a dark and smelly dungeon. The hours were long in that dreadful darkness. The stench of rottenness stuck to my hair immediately. While still feeling the burning of the lashes on my back, fear approached me slowly and stood in front of me with a torch illuminating the walls around me.

"What do you want from me? Why do you have me here? Answer me, I want to get out, let me out!" I screamed until I choked on my own saliva, until I ended up coughing and whining. The smelly, cracked-faced soldier laughed loudly, with a diabolical laugh, and approached me covering me with his stale breath.

"Don't hurt me" I begged, but he pounced on me. He licked my neck and my face. He touched my breasts in a grotesque way while I dodged him by moving my head from side to side, asking him not to hurt me. I implored, I don't know how many times, for him not to hurt me, however, my cries were useless because with a scream, the bearded savage paralyzed me by tearing my dress. He turned to the door and placed the torch on a hoop illuminating the earthen prison halfway. As he turned to me, his body became larger, his eyes darker, and his laughter more cruel. He grabbed me by the hair twisting my head back, and I knew the beginning of living in hell. I felt his hands on my breasts; massaging them brutally; then they went down to my buttocks and his mouth searched for mine with despair. I felt his erect member because he forced me to touch it. I felt it inside me... I screamed... I screamed as loud as I could but nobody heard me. Without any compassion he made me bend before him and did what he wanted with me and when he got tired, he left me in the gloominess of that foul dungeon.

For several days I endured the constant rapes of this big and barbaric man. I guessed the hours by the food left at the entrance, fruit in the morning and chickpea soup in the afternoon, but I didn't eat. I had a knot in my throat and in my stomach that didn't allow me to take any food. I barely drank water. The routine of the raping began at nightfall.

The last time I was abused, he couldn't finish inside me so he stuck a broomstick in my intimate areas. That made him finish over his pants. He left, leaving me like a wounded animal. That night, nauseated and in pain, I curled up and in my loneliness, I could not understand the reason for my misfortunes. It was the first time I wanted to die.

To my surprise, the morning after my last rape, the door opened, this time wide-open. The woman dressed in black with her eyes lined by the dark of the *kohl*[15] the woman who would bring me the food let me out of that stench into a small courtyard, I could not walk very well. My insides were sore; I had dried blood between my legs, and I could feel the semen stuck to my buttocks and my pubis. My custodian took me to the laundry area to wash me. As she poured bowls of fragrant and warm water over me, her voice said, "You must be strong, the body forgets, try to keep hope alive. Come on, let me clean you, don't cry anymore because tears and screams are of no use here, save your energy instead. I have to take care of you, let me do my job." I let myself be helped; it was a long bath and, at times, accompanied by a sweet melody.

When the woman with the niqab began to wash my hair, I also began to hum inwardly her song that spoke of love and the past; the one who bathed me chanted like a prayer to scare away the ghosts. I knew that song. I had sung it before... I don't know when, but I repeated again and again: "always by your side, keep me with you, never leave my

---

[15]*Kohl: Cosmetic made of a galena base with other ingredients, used to darken eyelids.*

sight. When I say love, my heart is soothed."

I sang with tears as regular companions, with fear possessing me stealthily, with my eyes closed to concentrate on reproducing the smell of Ahmed, that sweet smell that made me smile nights ago. My mind traveled through Abba's studio, it sailed around its corners and caressed its guava-colored walls, and I imagined the water purifying me by taking away the bad, the dirty and the impure. Finished with the bath, the woman wrapped my beaten body and led me to a cabin full of rooms. The air hit my cheeks along the way. I was hunched over by uncertainty. With my head down, I saw how to my left the golden dome of a mosque reflected over a puddle of clear water. Then we entered a large room without window equipped with lined cots.

The woman sat me in a chair, shut the doors and slowly began to brush my hair. Then she dried my body and rubbed oils on me, starting with my feet. The touch of her hands made me feel good, her way of massaging my body reassured me instead of repelling me. I knew that someone from my past had spoiled me like this, perhaps my mother. As the woman in the niqab with eyes delineated by the kohl exerted pressure on my sore spots, my mind opened like a cherry blossom in spring. Then I saw a woman with fine features and a wide smile; her green eyes gave me peace, she caressed my hair and rubbed with her soft hands those same oils that smelled of sandalwood. I had seen her before in those short flashes when intermittent images appeared and then gave way to migraines.

My companion prepared some poultices to reduce the inflammation of my bitten skin. She covered them with leaves that produced a slight heat, wrapped my flesh in a dark robe and left me alone for a moment, returning with a cup of tea. During that wait, I felt cold, but the cold was not of the body but of the soul. In those days I didn't see anyone else but the woman. I had perceived very distant voices in the night; the voices came from the same corridor where I was. Late in the afternoon, the woman with the niqab arrived with a plate of chickpea soup, fresh bread and a cup of tea. She looked at me surprised that the morning tray was almost full. I felt the reproach in her eyes and was able to beg, "keep me company for a few minutes, please." She left, closing the door behind her.

Slowly and painfully the days turned into nights, the nights into months; the months were too long to bear. After my arrival, two months before *Ramadan*[16] I wanted to end my life, but divine providence did not let it happen. I swallowed some gunpowder that I had stolen , I don't remember how. There are parts of the journey that I have forgotten over the years. What I am sure of is that it was a spoonful of black powder that in microseconds overwhelmed me with stomach pains, sweats, and cramps. I know Khadija found me in the backyard where the laundry was. I saw her with my lost gaze, and with a halo of voice that sounding pleading, I asked her to let me die. Mercy stood in

---

[16]*Ramadán: Ninth month of the lunar year when Muslims observe strict fasting.*

the way of my wishes, disappearing twisted and flooded by the smoke of a gleaming garlic-scented vomit rising from my bowels. Distorted faces added to the woman's who, in her attempts to save me, forced bowls of water and milk into my esophagus. Khadija's fingers dug through the dark tunnel of my throat to induce more vomiting. My attempt to escape ended in a cascade of green water and intermittent delirium for several days.

Ahmed Bakri was thousands of kilometers from Samira, witnessing deaths in Kobanî and Qamishli where a very high price was paid against the Islamic State. The chain of gunshots that inhabited him and his two companions for weeks ceased after a confrontation of almost three months. The terror of the Islamic State that by waving its flag made the citizens tremble, now quickly withdrew leaving two cities submerged in darkness and decay.

In his travels, Ahmed reported on the advances or setbacks of Bashar's government and the policies for refugees in Israel, Turkey, Jordan, and Iraq for their relocation or asylum. War always had one tragedy or another for him: mutilated friends, disappeared or dead, grenade blasts, bombs, drones and planes that did not give him a break. He spent six months coming and going from one place to another; calling people and recording stories in faraway places where war ravaged everything in its path. He reported a naked truth that the rest of the world was forgetting in the most desolate indifference. Syria still needed help, but nobody cared. There were days when he felt very despondent and the idea of applying for asylum became stronger, especially because he was sure that he had found love with Samira whom he missed deeply.

At the end of his journey in Qamishli, accompanied by his two inseparable partners in crime, insomnia and the seat of his cream-colored BMW, he thought of her again; the frightened young woman with no memory whom he rescued from the Al-Ramtha hospital in Irbid. Samira was always in his mind, as was the impotence that ate away at him for having left her alone. He returned to Zaatari, but first passed through Amman, he left his work at the television station.

Anxious, he reviewed the talk they had the last time he saw her, adding new arguments to his conversation. Every kilometer until Mafraq went slowly even though the speedometer indicated he was going several miles above the allowed speed limit.

When he arrived at the camp, everything seemed the same, the big registration tent at the entrance was still in the same place and the guards he had seen months before had the same routine. He asked to visit Samira but was told she was missing. Ahmed could not believe it. Samira had nowhere to go, she knew no one but him. Could she have recovered her memory during the time they were separated? he thought, upset.

"She must be here, let me pass!" he shouted. But the guard's answer was definitive.

"She is not here. She left. She's no longer in this camp," rebuked the guard, in an agitated tone.

"When did she leave? Did she leave a note, a number for Ahmed Bakri?"

The guard, losing his patience, raised his voice, articulating a "no" that rumbled in his ears like another war bomb. Ahmed quickly got into the BMW and once inside, a scream of helplessness was heard within the confined space of the cabin followed by his hand slapping the steering wheel. He started the car and decided to go around the camp, waiting for an opportunity to sneak into the TW68 tent that was designated to Samira the day he took her to UNHCR. He realized his idea was senseless. The camp was impenetrable as it was enclosed by a tight barbed wire fence. He felt a knot in his throat as if it were a fist clinging to his neck.

For him, the carnage on the battlefields was not the worst, nor the famine or needs of Syrian refugees; not even the bleakness of organ trafficking. Nothing compared to the idea that Samira could have been abused, exploited or sold. At a time when the war in his country aroused all sorts of mixed feelings, any misfortune was possible.

His body could not endure that thought and he threw up the coffee he had ingested an hour before on the desert floor. He felt a twinge in his temple and then a headache that he could not subdue, and he lay down on the seat of his car. He spent the night parked near the wire fence, the furthest away from the highway so as not to be seen. His intention was to enter Zaatari, the next day anyway he could.

He felt exhausted, he wanted to rest, however, it was useless trying to fall asleep. Throughout the night he was visited by the ghosts of battle, by the loud blasts of grenades and bullets, by the collapse of buildings, and by a parade of dismembered bodies crawling to reach his feet. The raw and bloody memory of the faces he had left unburied in other cities awoke him from that vicious nightmare after the first hours of dawn. With tears in his eyes and the sour taste of bile in his mouth, he decided to sneak under the wire fence. He stealthily managed to blend in with the people of Zaatari.

He walked, looking for the TW68 tent. When he found himself in front of it, he caught the attention of the woman who was embroidering sitting on a mattress full of threads and fabric. He asked for Samira but the woman, who seemed to be possessed by the continuous stitching exercise, did not flinch. Ahmed insisted by raising his voice and again mentioned Samira's name. Then, as if awakening from a trance, the woman introduced herself as Malak and immediately left the tent to meet him.

"Samira is not with us, she disappeared. Who are you?"

"My name is Ahmed Bakri, I'm a journalist and Samira's friend. Do you know how she disappeared?"

"One morning she left for the medical center and never came back. They say that a man took her when she saved a little girl from being hurt and instead, they took her. Some people went to her aid, but it was too late. We are second-class citizens. Everyone is silent. Many women and girls have disappeared but nobody does anything. If they can't deny the evils, they say they are working with the authorities to make the camp safer, but it's not true. Near the highway, I have seen some men stop to negotiate with parents the sale of their girls. They come from Mafraq to prowl the wire fence near the border and spend long hours there observing the movement in here. Being a woman is dangerous. There is no security," Malak finished, as she returned inside the tent and resumed her embroidery work.

Ahmed thanked her for talking to him. Malak's words cut him deeply. He perceived that the Syrians of Zaatari felt alone and lost and that the world mocked them in a cruel way. He realized that Malak was a young woman, but one that had aged twenty years. Her words denoted a mode of survival rather than of living. He immediately walked away along Souk Street.

Ahmed observed a group of girls running to one of the nine camp schools where they studied during the morning shift. He knew Zaatari, he had done some reporting on the growth of the camp and knew by heart the names of the schools and their schedules. Girls always go to school first and then return to help out with the chores, and the boys go in the afternoon.

He hastily tried to find a clue in the Al-Ameed café and the Daara Al-Balad tailoring shop, but he got no answers, only more stories of stress, nervousness, frustration, and violence.

Devastated, he thought he had lost his magic as a reporter

and, overwhelmed, he went to the other side of the camp where he had left the car. He had a hard time crawling under the fence even though he cut the metal with his little Work Champ XL pocket knife to have a space to slide down. The spikes hurt his arms and back as he tried to get out towards the car.

The humid and cool October weather hit the camp air again. The night fell slowly, and Ahmed headed for Amman. Behind him again were Zaatari and its people, continuing to fall prey to routine and their terrible fortune in a long rectangle of the desert that grew with time. Abba's writings in the newspaper and the videos telling the story of that girl with no memory whom he promised to rescue from the refugee camp were useless. The earth had swallowed her up, and he was tired of fighting the war and the ghosts.

In November, Ahmed decided to give himself a chance and accepted a job offer from TF1 Channel in France. Even then, far away already, the smell of war haunted him. The sad and mutilated images, which in his dreams remained present, were confused with the memory of Samira's green eyes that would not leave him alone. Meanwhile, the deep crisis, resulting from the confrontations of Bashar and the rebels, added to the infiltrated, divided Syria more and more and became unsustainable for those who asked for refuge in other countries. Isolated attacks were taking place on the streets of Europe, and they were slowly taking over some of its cities. It was 2016 and the world was wounded to death just like him. This he would write to Abba sometime later. The feeling of loneliness and mourning that Ahmed's letters conveyed to Abba, with whom he maintained a fluid epistolary communication, despite the distance, was recorded in his column in the Jordan Times newspaper, which he had called 'A Duel in the Sun.'

After my suicide attempt, the Wali had ordered Ramee, the man who raped me, to bend my pride by making me the cleaner of the communal house bathrooms and the soldiers' barracks. For hours I cleaned shit, the smells of urine and the spittle left in the toilets by the soldiers. Armed only with a bucket and a brush, I crawled on my hands and knees through the bathrooms every day, being beaten and abused by combatants who came in just to make fun of me for being a woman. At first, I wanted to empty my insides when I perceived the dirt and pestilence, but I overcame it and drew strength from weakness. Dirty, sweaty and with the constant smell of excrement, I saw that spring had arrived. The trees outside the room indicated that green was cornering the grey trunks with its vibrant color. Then came summer with its imposing heat and finally autumn, full of sonorous winds and black smoke, near the communal house, from the burning of tires due to the continuous confrontations with the *peshmerga*[17] soldiers.

I spent my days and nights locked up and surrounded by high walls that separated me from everything I knew out there. As I cleaned, I listened to the caliph's men extolling themselves for the scenes of horror they were carrying

---

[17] *Peshmergas: Term used by Kurds to refer to the armed Kurd combatants.*

out in France and the attacks they provoked in Turkey to increase recruitment. They celebrated the death of six guards on the northern and northwestern border between Syria and Jordan, they congratulated each other on the attacks on the United States, the beheadings of American and British journalists, the attack on all the allies of the North American regime, and supported all events that filled with unrest and turmoil the sinful societies according to the ideas of the Wali, the blessed Muhammad, the great caliph.

Fear and sadness dwelt not only in me but in the new women they had abducted. They were *Yazidis*[18]. Abductions, rapes, confinement, punishments and being sold in cages, were our daily bread. I never knew the fate of the white girls, those who arrived with me in the truck; neither did I see the yellow-eyed girl, nor the others. After the beating in the courtyard, their presence dissipated like the colors of dawn at noon. I didn't know if they were sold or killed. Little by little the faces disappeared and were supplanted by new faces and different moods. One day the cots were invaded by bodies and the next day they were empty, impregnated with a dark aura.

Zafira found me several times curled up in the corners of the bathrooms after the insults and the blows. Patiently and in secret she bathed me, gave me something to eat and dressed me in new clothes. The other women who were assigned to the service and were distributed in the kitchen, laundry and cleaning avoided me by making rude

---

[18]*Yazidi: Community that lives mostly in the Nineveh Province.*

comments about my smell and my presence. All this made me feel more alone than ever. Zafira and Khadija were the only ones who took care of me and did it in secret.

One autumn afternoon, when the chores were finished, I sat down in front of the fountain at the entrance of the house. I was dizzy and I thought it was because I hadn't eaten. My belly hurt, it was a sharp pain that little by little took my breath away. Then a river of blood flowed from between my legs and a lump fell to the ground. I got scared. It had the shape of a baby. I was going to touch it and I saw how its little hands were closing inside the bloody membrane. I got up and wrapped the fetus in my double veiled hijab. I walked with difficulty to the kitchen and there I found Khadija, who once again, saved me from dying.

I remember falling to my knees. Blood ran down my thighs, leaving thick drops on the floor. I asked for help and saw Khadija, her face illuminated by the fire of the cauldron, with a tender and compassionate look. Her warm hands held my body so as not to let me fall completely. She asked another woman in the kitchen to bring a bench, sat me against the wall, made me drink fresh water, and moistened my face with a piece of cloth. She took me to the rooms where we rested and laid me on my cot. She left the room and came back with water and towels. Her restless breathing made me a little nervous, but her hands on my belly calmed me down when I knew that if I died, I would not be alone, that my soul would receive a prayer like for that little being who, untimely, came out of my entrails.

While she washed my body and cleaned my hands, Khadija recited a prayer to her Peacock Angel, to *Melek Taus*[19] and accompanied her prayers with the ringing of small bells from necklace hidden in her black *abaya*[20]. Khadija never ceased to be Yazidi. Even though she took an oath in Islam she still believed in the god of her ancestors and was sure that he would save me.

My body began to shake uncontrollably and sweat profusely. I became dizzy and the voice that once seemed docile now became deep and distant. With that change of voice, I began to travel. I traveled to Aleppo. I went through the corners that my memory had hidden from reality. I saw my family, hugged my father and smiled with my mother and sister. I visited the hospital where I worked as a nurse and talked to Keled, the boy owner of an old soul. I returned to the Latakia flower festival and bathed in the Levantine sea, whose crystalline waters furrowed me and allowed me to hear the crashing of its waves on the horizon. Little by little the sound of the sea turned into an imposing rough water where its foam became dust covering the floor of the Irbid clinic with corpses. Strong arms held me, the trembling of my body calmed down and the burning of my skin, due to the fever of the infection that killed the baby, gave way, as did my willingness to resist the desire not to live.

I felt that I resurrected from the crests of the blue sea and the immensity of its waves. Suddenly there were no more

---

[19]*Melek-Taus:the 'Peacock Angel', is the Arabic name for the main Yazidi deity.*
[20]*Abaya: Simple, loose dress used by some women in the Muslim world.*

blurred memories, life returned as good news returns from the soul: slow, happy, whole, pious, and brave. I no longer contemplated myself with pity or fear, because there she was with her red hair like tongues of fire, she was again, fighting for my life to the death.

I awoke from death and overcame the misfortune when I saw Khadija's eyes again resting on mine. Her face with thick lips and wide nose was a phosphorescent watercolor that smiled with relief at the fact that I had not left this world. I never understood the joy with which Khadija received me. Death, for any of us, was better than being deprived of freedom. However, she did not conceive it. I remember she said to me: "Samira, your soul traveled to beautiful places, you are well now, now is the right time to get out of here. I didn't understand her words, I was confused like when Ahmed found me in the hospital of Al-Ramtha. She realized this and emphasized, "It's time to flee Samira! We're ready to flee now!"

Khadija and Zafira had converted to Islam after the Ramadan celebration. The event was public and was attended by all of us who lived in the communal house. Although they could convert in private, it was advisable not only to follow the rules of the Caliph, but also to convince others, including the family of the Wali of the Islamic State, that the surrender and conversion were total and sincere. Khadija and Zafira recited their testimony of faith aloud. "La ilaha illa Allah, Muhammad rasul Allah", by pronouncing the Shahada they accepted Islam as their true religion and the

Qur'an as the literal word of God revealed to the prophet Muhammad. We, the other women, put our hands to our breasts, bowed our heads and pray for the world, for our people, for health and for ourselves under a fierce silence. Our eyes closed as we listened to the Shahada and then glanced towards the sun.

While I toured the communal house cleaning toilets and sunken in my own pain, the two of them had been planning a future. Secretly the two had made a sum of money from the sales of the forgiveness cards the caliph sold to the average Muslims. They had also acquired two guns that they hid in two small chests and had a few rounds of ammunition hidden behind the kitchen oven. Zafira was the Wali's beloved, she was a beautiful young woman who had left Samarra with him with the idea of forming a family. But he became her nightmare while the people made him a giant. Once they arrived in Mosul, after the first year, her happiness disappeared, and it became a time of remorse and anxiety. When she learned that she was pregnant, she had to make an effort so that the baby on the way would have a future far from the cruelty of his father and his erroneous and bloodthirsty ideals.

Fortune had smiled on Khadija just as she arrived at the communal house, her yellow eyes met those of Zafira and she immediately took her under her wings with the permission of the caliph. Zafira's instinct did not fail her, Khadija was her eyes, ears and strength in moments of weakness. Together they planned the escape. The patience of these two women bore fruit and when the opportunity presented itself, they decided to take me with them. Zafira did it as redemption for her husband's sins and chose to save our lives along with hers. Those had been her words in revealing and including Khadija in her escape plans.

I still felt pain in my belly. As I passed my hands over it, I felt relieved but empty. There was no one else in the room, all the women were doing their chores. I heard the squeal of the door when it opened and I saw Zafira. She sat down in the only chair available as an accessory in the middle of the worn-out cots on the floor and told me: "Let's get out of here Samira. We have to get out of here because it's not just my well-being anymore." She hugged her belly, and I could see a lump protruding from her abaya. "Everything is planned. You must play the best role in your life. Your luck, mine, and Khadija's depend on it."

I didn't know the exact plan, but I wanted to get out of this hell. At the exact time that Zafira told me, Khadija came for me. She brought a mujahideen uniform in her hands and made me change. She put me in a turban and asked me to escort her to the kitchen. Once there she handed me a roll of money and a forgiveness card signed by the caliph. She instructed me to keep it safe and indicated me to go to the main exit and wait for them there. She kept two more bundles of money and some documents in her backpack and tied the gun to her thigh with a white cloth ribbon. She covered a hole behind the gas stove and pushed me to the exit.

The great Wali was out of town, he had gone to the town of Tal Afar to support his army against the Kurdish peshmerga, who were fighting to expel them from their territory. We would use his absence and vulnerability at this moment to leave.

The minutes waiting for Zafira and Khadija were an eternity. My muscles were tense, and my heart beat like a runaway horse. I was afraid that during the wait other mujahideen would arrive and discover me. My fears came true when I saw Ramee heading towards me, his long steps seemed to reach me, the wrinkles of his sunburnt face became deeper and his eyes were burning more knowing him soon by my side. Zafira and Khadija cut him off with a firm and forceful voice.

"Ramee!" called Khadija. "I am going with the lady to the market before it closes, she has ordered the *mujahideen*[21] to escort us."

"Don't delay," ordered Ramee. "Curfew will be called in a few hours. There are many Kurdish and Shiite enemies wishing to cause trouble. It is not safe to be out, much more so in your state." As I listened to him, I thought of the caliph and his fury when he would learn that his wife had escaped with two slaves. If we were caught, the Wali and Ramee would have no mercy on us.

"You, move, and open the gate!" Ramee roared. "I leave them in your care. If anything happens to the lady, they'll tear your eyes out."

---

[21]*Mujahideen: Fundamentalist Islamic combatant.*

With my stomach burning, I did what I had to do. I summed up the courage and walked tightly because of the stiffness of my muscles towards the exit along with Zafira and Khadija acting as their *mahram*[22]. A few steps ahead, turning the corner, we took a taxi. My face was still covered as male militants do when I got into the vehicle, I wore my black plaid headscarf covering part of my mouth and nose. Once in the seat Zafira ordered the driver to go to Mosul's exit. He looked at me, and I nodded without saying a word, insistently tapping the door, pointing towards the exit to Erbil with my index finger.

We lived northwest of the city where nearly ten citadels had been besieged by the regiments of the caliph. We knew it would be very difficult to get out of there, but we commended ourselves to our God and let Him once again decide our future.

The taxi took us through bombed streets, destroyed citadels, and we saw people running for cover before hearing the alarm that would put them in danger again.

The vehicle zigzagged several times avoiding bumping into stray cats. We were lucky, there was no enemy to stop us. I couldn't believe it, the emotion seized my face, the muscles in my face loosened. As we left Mosul for Erbil, we saw a checkpoint bearing the black flag of the Islamic State. Several cars were being inspected, some drivers were beaten and women were dragged into a truck. A short and

---

[22]*Mahram: A chaperone, could be a woman or a man with blood ties. In case of the Islamic State, anyone can be appointed as such.*

corpulent mujahideen approached us pointing his gun at us and shouted, "Identification!"

The taxi driver showed his, he looked nervous, his hand was shaking. The mujahideen with an authoritative voice asked for his forgiveness card. Startled, the driver looked at us and began to stutter. I saw Khadija raise her skirt to her thigh and opened my eyes. Zafira noticed my nervousness and squeezed Khadija's hand quelling her actions. Then she removed the veil covering her face and showed her documents. "We are going to Kalak, brother," said Zafira enveloping him in her warm voice and blue eyes. The mujahideen withdrew with a bow and allowed us to pass, alerting the others of the urgency. As we crossed the checkpoint, the curfew alarm rang. The deafening sound reached us, letting us know that the conflict in western Mosul would not end soon, that the Islamic State was seeking to destroy everything and that its arm was advancing like a tsunami, annihilating men, women, the elderly and children in its wake. Its resonance gave us goosebumps under the dark clothes that covered our bodies. I felt it in the glances of my two companions, and I saw it in my own reflected in the rearview mirror of the taxi.

I could sense the fear in the eyes of our driver who, in astonishment, discovered that I was a woman when I dropped my headscarf down to my neck almost on reaching Kalak. Further down the road, as we crossed Kawraban and reached Turaq, I raised my eyes and saw a sign in thick white letters posted on the road reading 'towards Erbil'. I raised my hands to heaven and laughed. I laughed with a mixture of uncertainty and exclaimed with all the strength of my being: "We are already out of the communal house! Out of the confinement! Out of the stench of urine and shit! Out of the hands of the mujahideen! Far from Ramee and his rotten breath, from his rough tongue! We are for the first time on the way to freedom!"

The laughter was contagious, Zafira and Khadija freed themselves from the double veil they had been wearing, as had I, for a long time and lay down letting the color of their hair be seen. The taxi driver also laughed as his eyes shed tears.

Through the rearview mirror I see the faces of Khadija and Zafira whose eyes of different features and colors show relief; hope has rejuvenated them both. They laugh with the freshness of a renewed youth in their expressions.

As we cross the intersection of 60 Meter Street, the bitter life and savage treatment we faced during the war becomes a thing of the past. The Al-Maidan neighborhood and the communal house are far away. Erbil receives us without the squawking of the curfew alarm... it frees us from a confinement where sanity and dignity had no place. In our immediate present there is only a new sky, turning silver as night falls. Now all that remains is to gather faith, because faith is what keeps you grounded and what lets you fly.

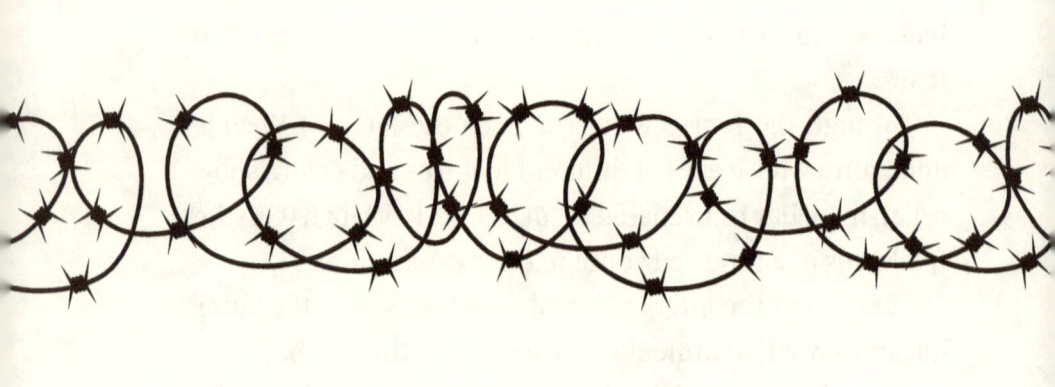

www.ingramcontent.com/pod-product-compliance
Lightning Source LLC
Chambersburg PA
CBHW050758250626
47155CB00005B/2121